The Irish Storm

Birth of the Republic of Ireland

1918 - 1923

The Irish Storm

Birth of the Republic of Ireland

1918 - 1923

J Walter Ring

Dedication

Peg and Bob Spinozzi

Bessie and Nellie McAnley

Walter and Margaret (née Ludden) Ring

Joe and John (Jack) Ring

Preface

In 1169 the Normans of England invaded a decentralized Ireland, and thus began more than 800 years of English political and military involvement in that country. The island was divided into small monarchies, and the Normans attacked one kingdom after another. The nature of Ireland's political organization, small territories, martial traditions, difficult terrain and climate, and lack of urban infrastructure meant that attempts to assert Crown authority were slow and expensive.

The English Crown did not make another attempt to further subjugate Ireland until the end of the War of Roses in 1488. England's attempts to impose the new Protestant religion were rejected by both the Gaelic and Norman-Irish. In 1534, the Earl of Kildare, Silken Thomas, was determined to defend the traditional autonomy and Catholicism, and that marked the beginning of the Tudor conquest of Ireland from 1534 to 1603. In 1541 Henry VIII declared himself King of Ireland.

England's attempts to either conquer or assimilate both the Irish lordships and the Gaelic territories into the Kingdom of Ireland was the basis for continuing warfare marked by the Crown policies of sending thousands of English and Scottish Protestant settlers to displace both Old English and native Catholic landholders. Gaelic Ireland was finally defeated 1601, which resulted in the collapse of the Gaelic system and the beginning of Ireland's history as part of the British Empire.

During the 17th century, this division between a Protestant landholding minority and a dispossessed Catholic majority intensified, and conflict between them became a recurrent theme in Irish history. Domination of Ireland by the Protestant Ascendancy was reinforced after two periods of religious war--in 1641-52 and in 1689-91. After that, political power rested almost exclusively in the Protestant Ascendancy, while the majority Catholics suffered severe political and economic privation under the Penal Laws.

The Penal Laws included:

- Exclusion of Catholics from holding such public offices as judge, MP, solicitor, jurist, barrister, civil servant, sheriff, or town councillor.
- No Catholic could vote or be elected to office.
- A ban against owning land was imposed on Catholics.
- Catholics could not lease land for longer than 31 years, and rent was to equal two-thirds of the yearly value of the land.
- Catholics were not allowed to hold arms, be members of the armed forces, or own a horse

worth more than £5.

- If a Catholic landholder died, his estate could not be passed to the eldest son unless that son was a Protestant. Otherwise, it was to be shared by all the surviving sons.
- A ban was imposed preventing intermarriage between Catholics and Protestants.
- Catholic could not be an orphan's guardian.
- Catholics were barred from living in many provincial towns.
- Catholic clergy were to be registered and were required to take an oath of loyalty, but friars, monks, church hierarchy, and Jesuits were to be exiled.
- No cleric could wear distinguishing clothes.
- Places of worship could not have a steeple or display a cross.
- Catholics and dissenters were required to pay tithes to the Anglican Church of Ireland, which was the established church.
- Catholics could not establish schools or send their children abroad for education.

On January 1, 1801, Ireland became part of a new United Kingdom of Great Britain and Ireland. The catastrophic Great Potato Famine struck Ireland in 1845, resulting in over a million deaths from starvation and disease and in millions of refugees fleeing the country, mostly to America. Irish attempts to break away from England continued until Ireland eventually won the Home Rule Act of 1914; however, this act was suspended at the outbreak of World War I.

This is the background for "The Irish Storm."

Acknowledgments

Thank you to my long-time editor Carolyn Woolston for her experience, expertise, and insights and to Casey Dawes for formatting. Thanks to my cousins Peg Spinozzi and Tracy Inwood for their help in researching our family history and providing the photographs for this book. Thank you also to my beta readers, Bambi and Ken Rathman, Dyana Hulgan, Peg Spinozzi, Tracy Inwood, and Joe Ring for their time and comments.

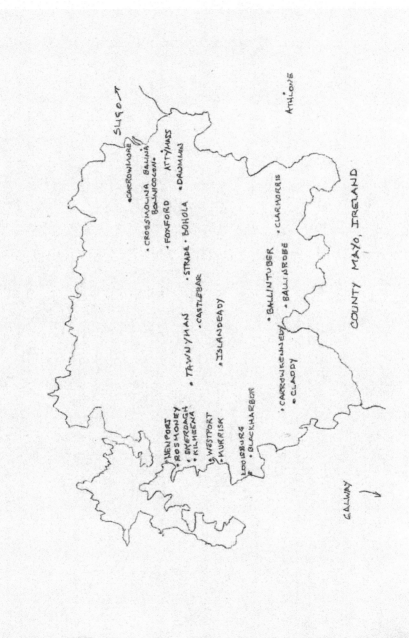

COUNTY MAYO, IRELAND

Chapter One

The Great War

Ronssoy, Northeastern France
March 20, 1918

"What's that?" the young private asked.

Sergeant Emerson 'Bud' Ryan glanced his way. "What?"

"Listen ... between the artillery bursts. It sounds like a dog."

Ryan gave a tired sigh. "Sullivan, is this the first time you've heard a dog barkin'?"

The private's eyes widened. "Out there? What's a dog doing out there? How can it survive?" He climbed up onto the firing step, then peeked over the muddy parapet through the barbed wire at the bleak, bare landscape of no man's land.

Sergeant Ryan grabbed him. "Hey, keep your bloody head down!"

Suddenly a bullet ricocheted off the boy's helmet and sent him sliding back down the embankment onto the muddy trench floor. Only Bud's grip on his uniform kept him from falling on his face into the muck covering the duckboard planking. He gritted his teeth, picked up the helmet, inspected the silver crease in the blue-green paint, and handed it back to the reedy blond private. "Put this back on and keep your head down, or it's St. Peter you'll be meetin'. Didn't they warn you about snipers before they sent you out here?"

"How can they see me through all that barbed wire?"

"They see movement. Keep out of sight."

"Sorry, Sergeant." Private Sullivan began to scrape the thick mud off his leggings and boots.

"Don't be apologizin'", Bud growled. "Just be more careful." He looked up at the colorless sky. It was the same grey as the earth in no man's land, the walls of the trench, the duckboard planking, the muddy water, and the men. It was the first day of spring, he remembered. Maybe we're done with the snow and ice. *Maybe we're done with this whole endless, bloody mess.* But he knew they weren't.

He blew out a long breath. Spring would bring the

stench of raw sewage, stagnant water, and rotting bodies. At least it would be something different.

He pulled his overcoat tighter to ward off the misty chill. He'd keep these men alive if it was the last thing he ever did. He sighed again, and through the sound of random artillery fire he heard someone sloshing toward him through the zig-zag trenches. Because of the stalemate, the armies on both sides had learned to dig trenches in sawtooth patterns to give soldiers cover if their position was overrun.

The runner rounded the last corner, and Bud pushed himself away from the trench wall. "What is it, son?"

"Sergeant Ryan," the young man panted, "there's an emergency meeting at the command post. Lieutenant Dawes wants you there."

Bud nodded. *Wonder what the hell this is all about at this hour.* He followed the runner to the communications trench and then back to the support trenches. The eight-foot walls were high enough that he didn't need to crouch as he slogged after the runner, even though he was taller than most of his men

The command post was a cave dug into the wall of the trench farthest from no man's land. Other sergeants were gathered at the entrance, waiting to duck into the meeting. When Bud entered, he saluted Lieutenant Dawes, the officer in command, and noted the warmth of the cave and the aroma of brewing tea, a welcome change from the cold and the stench of the trenches.

"Sergeant Ryan reportin', sir."

The officer returned his salute. "At ease, Bud. Have some tea." He motioned to the tiny cook stove and the assortment of metal cups on his desk. "And it's your squad's turn to man the listening post in your sector tonight," he added, wiping his wire-rimmed glasses. He was clean-shaven, and his uniform was neater than those of the sergeants now filing in. He hadn't been out rolling around in the muck as Bud and his squad of Irish Fusiliers had. Dawes was new to the 16th Irish Division of the British Expeditionary Force. Their last commanding officer had been killed a month ago during the Battle of Cambrai. Bud liked Dawes, but the man wasn't battle-tested yet.

He poured himself some tea and warmed his hands around the cup.

"Is everybody here?" Dawes shouted. "Let's get on with it."

All conversation ceased as the lieutenant began to speak. "The high command thinks the Germans are planning a large-scale spring offensive. As you know, the Americans have now entered the war. In another month the first hundred thousand troops should be taking positions with us, so this spring is Germany's last chance to have a go at us and end the war before the Americans arrive."

"Would you be knowin' when the Jerries are goin' to attack?" one sergeant shouted.

"We don't, but we need to be ready. How are the new replacements doing?"

Bud spoke up. "One of our lads stuck his head up to take a peek at the landscape, and a sniper creased his helmet for him."

"Is he all right?"

"He's fine, and now he's a lot smarter."

The other sergeants chuckled.

"Be prepared for an attack in the next couple of days," Dawes continued. "We're moving more reserve troops into the forward trench and more into the reserve trenches. Deploy them to the best advantage. More machine gun squads are arriving with the new infantry. Show them the best positions in your area. We expect the action to be along the entire front."

The men were silent.

"That should do it," the lieutenant said. "Cooperate with the units assigned to your flanks, and don't let any gaps develop. Dismissed."

Bud drained his cup, saluted Dawes, and slogged back to his trench to address the men.

"Hey, mates, we have listenin'-post duties tonight. Sullivan, you think you can get out in the sap and not get shot?"

"What's a sap, Sarge?"

Bud closed his eyes and shook his head. "It's the trench dug out into no man's land. Go out to the end of the trench and be listenin'. Don't stick your head up, just listen."

"What am I listenin' for?"

"Listen for mechanical equipment movin' around on the other side. When that stops and the artillery goes silent, get back here and tell me."

"Right, sir."

"The rest of you, listen up. The generals think there will be an attack in the next couple of days because the Germans are hopin' to break through us before the Americans get here. Go to supply and bring up all the ammunition and food you can carry. McGann, the reserves have a couple of Vickers machine gun crews comin' with them. Tonight, after dark, send a couple of men out to cut holes in our barbed wire and set the machine gun crews opposite the breaks. Tell them to hold their fire until the first Germans funnel through the gaps, then let them have it."

"All right, Sarge."

The fresh soldiers jogged through the communications trenches and fanned out in the forward trench in both directions. As they trotted past him, Bud looked into their young faces. Most avoided looking at him, but he saw the fear in their eyes. He stopped one soldier and asked who his sergeant was.

"McKenna, sir."

Bud and Corporal McGann moved on down the ditch, and when they found Sergeant McKenna, Bud stuck out his hand. "I'm Sergeant Bud Ryan."

"Ian McKenna," the other man said.

"Does your unit have any experience?"

McKenna nodded. "We were in the trenches during Third Ypres. Lost twenty percent of our men, but the replacements have had some trainin'."

"They're just lads," Bud observed.

"They'll grow up fast enough. What's goin' on here?"

"We're expectin' a general attack soon." He looked up at the darkening sky. "It's gettin' late. Have your troops eaten?"

"They fed us before sendin' us out."

"Good. Corporal McGann here will show you the tunnels where we sleep. My men will sleep the first shift, you can take the second. McGann will also show you where your lookouts can take up their stations."

* * *

Bud jolted upright, awakened by the sudden silence. *No artillery noise.* He sat up and listened, then scanned the tunnel. "McGann," he shouted. "Get everybody up. They're comin'."

The men rolled out of the shelter into the predawn darkness and fanned out along the trenches. Bud peered over the parapet and saw nothing, so he gripped his rifle and focused his hearing on the dark enemy trenches.

Suddenly, ten thousand artillery pieces and mortars spoke. A moment later, the British and French artilleries responded.

"Everyone back in the tunnels!" Bud shouted.

Artillery and mortar shells exploded around the trenches and on the earth covering the tunnels. The ground shook as the barrage went on and on, and the men braced themselves on the tunnel walls as the earth rocked.

Four hours later the bombardment and the close quarters began to tell on the huddled men. "We got to get out of here," someone yelled.

Bud braced himself in the tunnel exit and stuffed down his own growing anxiety. "Hold your positions," he shouted over the boom of explosions. "Get hold of yourselves! They'll be plenty to worry about real soon."

Another hour of artillery fire ended in an eerie calm. Bud listened to the silence for a moment and then yelled, "Everyone out of the tunnel! They're comin'!"

Other sections on both sides of his tunnel emptied at the same time. Soldiers moved up to the firing step, and thousands of German voices all screamed at once. Overhead, flares lit up no man's land as hundreds of dark shapes ran toward them.

Bud took aim at a shadow and fired. The Vickers crews opened up, and even though German soldiers were crumpling, some of their forward units reached the barbed wire. The first ones were shot and fell into the wire. Other soldiers stepped on their bodies to climb over.

The Fusiliers poured fire into the horde. After about twenty minutes, Bud realized his troops were being overwhelmed and ordered them into the reserve trenches.

But not quickly enough. German soldiers overran sections of the reserve and backup trenches. He emptied his rifle, then ordered his men to get out of the trenches and make for the town of Ronssoy.

He was the last man out of the reserve trench. German gunfire cut down the men running in front of him, and an artillery shell burst off to his right. But instead of the usual white smoke rising from the shell explosion, a yellow plume formed.

"Mustard gas!" he shouted. "Run to the left!"

He sprinted to his left, then stopped and pulled out his Bulldog revolver. He shot two enemy soldiers, and suddenly the scent of garlic reached his nostrils. He zig-zagged to the left and kept moving until something struck him and spun him to the ground. He tried to get up, but his left leg wouldn't work. He rose onto his right knee, fired his revolver until it was empty, and somehow got to his feet and tried to run.

The last thing he heard was an odd ringing in his ears.

* * *

His eyelids fluttered open to see the starched, winged coronets of two Sisters of Charity. "Where am I?"

One of the nuns bent over him. "You are in a French aid station," she said in heavily accented English.

He tried to sit up, but the pain in his hip was too great. When he sucked in his breath, his lungs hurt.

"Lie still, Sergeant."

He let his head fall back on the pillow. "What happened?" he muttered.

"You have been wounded," the nun replied. "And you inhaled some mustard gas. Your shoulder patch tells us you were with the Irish Division of the British Army," she continued, "but we don't know your unit."

"I'm with the 16th Division, 49th Brigade, 7th Royal Irish Fusiliers."

She turned to the other nun. "Sister Jacynthe, get the military liaison."

Bud closed his eyes and tried not to move. When he opened them, he found two French military officers with their distinctive kepis looking down at him.

"Sergeant Ryan?"

"That's me."

"How did you come to be here?"

"We were in the trenches protecting Ronssoy. The last thing I remember is being overrun by German soldiers. I ordered a retreat, and an artillery shell of mustard gas exploded, so I ordered my squad away from the gas cloud. Then I must have got hit because I fell to the ground, and when I tried to get up one of my legs wouldn't work. That's the last thing I remember."

"A bullet passed through your hip, Sergeant. And you inhaled some mustard gas."

"Will I be able to walk?"

"Yes, with some physical therapy. We are transferring you to a British unit, and from there you will be taken to England to recover. Your lungs will heal to some extent, but your breathing may bother you for some time."

"Why am I here in a French aid station?"

The two officers looked at each other. "There was a counterattack," one answered. "Two men from the 36th Ulster Division brought you in. The British aid stations were full, so they sent you to us.

I'll be damned. Saved by Ulster men. Who would guess Irish Protestants would be so helpful to a Catholic lad?

He dropped his head back onto his pillow. "When can I

get back to my unit?"

The captain hesitated. "I'm sorry, Sergeant. The 16th Division was all but wiped out in the spring offensive. Only a handful of you survived, and the unit no longer exists. If you recuperate enough to return to duty, you will be reassigned to another unit, but ..." He swallowed. "The doctors say you will not recover well enough."

Bud stared at him. *Not recover ...?* The words made no sense. "You mean I can't go back to the fightin'?"

The officer nodded and looked away. "That's right, son. You're not going back."

"Could I be havin' some paper and a pencil?" he asked finally. "I want to write home."

The captain turned to one of the nuns. "Sister?"

When the nun returned, she handed him a clipboard and a pencil. He positioned the paper so he could write in a half-reclining position and chewed on the end of the pencil for a long minute. He thought of all the times he'd wanted to write to Rose, all the things he'd wanted to say, but there'd been no time. It had taken him every minute of every day just trying to stay alive. Well, now he could say all those things. He could spill out his love for her in ways he couldn't in the trenches.

But when he lifted the pencil, he found he could only speak of ordinary things.

Dearest Rose,

I have good news and bad news. The good news is that I am coming home. The bad news is that I have been wounded. They are sending me to England to recover, and they say I will be there for a few months. I'll write to you as soon as I arrive, and please, please write back. I can face anything if I can hear your voice in my head.

Please, Rose.

Bud.

After five days, he could sit up, but with considerable pain. He was loaded onto a stretcher and transported to the French port of Dieppe, where he was transferred to a white hospital ship. When he arrived at Dover, he was carried into a hospital where he began rehabilitation.

Three months later he could walk on his own, and one evening he felt strong enough to sign out of the rehab unit for a short while. He dressed in his uniform and went looking for a tavern.

Chapter Two

Getting Ready

He found a pub with a red rose painted on the sign over the entrance. Rose's Tavern. Uniformed British soldiers were going in, so he decided to step in and have a pint with them.

The tavern was large and posh. The wood on the bar was polished mahogany that matched the wall paneling, and paintings of sports scenes hung on every wall. The seats at the bar and the surrounding tables were buff-colored leather, the carpet was thick and soft, and the air smelled of pipe smoke and sandalwood. He bellied up to the bar, ordered a beer, and tossed down a coin.

The bartender eyed his division patch and the medals on

his uniform. "Are you lost, Sarge?"

Bud stared at him. "No, just thought I'd be havin' a pint. Haven't had one in months."

The bartender filled a glass and slid it to him. Then a British soldier drinking with a group of uniformed noncommissioned officers leaned his elbow on the bar and sent him an unfriendly look.

"Well, blimey, look at this now," he sneered. "Behold, lads, we have one of the Sinn Fein boys here, and a big one at that. And look! He's taken the King's shilling." He narrowed his eyes. "Now, why would you be wearing that Irish uniform patch in a British pub?"

Bud held up his hand. "I'm not lookin' for trouble, mate. I just came in to have a quiet pint." He took a sip of his beer, leaned both elbows on the bar, and looked straight ahead.

"I saw you limping in, mick," the soldier said. "Did you hurt yourself running away from the war? The Times says the Irish troops are poor quality, and the British commanders could never count on them. Is that true?"

Bud took another sip and continued to stare straight ahead.

The soldier edged closer. "I'm talking to you, mick." He reached out and spun Bud around to face him, then saw he was looking into the barrel of Bud's Bulldog revolver.

"I limp because I was shot during the German offensive at the Somme," he said quietly. "I was fightin' off the Jerries so the fine English troops behind us had time to escape. Does that answer your question, *Private*?"

The soldier's eyes dropped to Bud's chest.

"And," Bud continued in an even tone, "I earned these medals at Loos and at Messines and at Passchendaele. Now if were you, mate, I'd be mindin' my own business."

Out of the corner of his eye he saw the bartender slowly bring up a sawed-off shotgun and aim it at him. Bud thumbed back the hammer on his revolver and gritted his teeth. "If I hear a loud noise," he said calmly, "I'll jerk my finger and put a bullet right through this man's head."

The bartender nodded. "I'll lower my shotgun if you release the hammer on that revolver."

Slowly Bud released the hammer, and the bartender lowered the shotgun barrel. "There's an Irish pub just around the corner, mick. I think we'd all be more comfortable if you decided to go drink with your mates. Why don't you go have a beer on me?" He tossed Bud's coin back at him.

Without hurrying, Bud lowered his revolver, finished his beer, and collected the coin. Then he murmured, "God save the King" and backed out of the tavern.

Five British soldiers followed him out onto the street, but when he reached into his pocket, they scrambled back inside. He limped on down the street, turned the corner, and spied a rickety wooden sign that read McGinty's Irish Pub. From inside he could hear singing and a piano banging out a familiar Irish tune, and he smiled.

McGinty's Irish Pub was much smaller than Rose's Tavern, and a good deal shabbier. The bar ran along one wall, and three dimly lit tables sat along the opposite wall. The tables were bare, the place smelled of corned beef and cabbage, the piano was out of tune, and the singers sounded drunk. Bud couldn't stop smiling. He felt right at home.

"Hey, lads," an exuberant voice shouted. "Looks like we've got one of the king's own here to visit us! You're not lost, are ya, Sergeant?"

The piano went silent, and all heads turned toward him. "Ah no, I'm not lost," Bud responded in his thickest Irish brogue. "I'm thinkin' I be among friends."

The piano player resumed his tune, and three men standing at the bar, all dressed in workingmen's clothes, invited Bud to join them. They retired to a table in the rear, where they each took a chair. "And, where you be from, biggun?" one of them asked.

"County Mayo. Westport, to be exact. Name's Emerson Ryan, but I go by Bud. I'm fresh from a military rehab center here."

The leader of the group, a tall, youngish man with curly red hair, extended his hand. "Paddy Timmons. On your left is Toby O'Hara, and Paul Lonergan is to your right." Bud shook their hands. Both O'Hara and Lonergan looked older, with lined faces and rough-looking hands.

"What are you doin' in Dover?" Paddy asked.

"Gettin' patched up before I head home. I was with the Wild Geese Division, the 16th Irish, and I got hit in France."

All at once the patrons and the piano went silent again, and everyone turned toward the entrance. Two helmeted British police officers stood in the doorway, scanning the tavern and slapping their nightsticks in their hands. "We're looking for a soldier, a sergeant," one said. "A big man with a limp. Just came out of Rose's Tavern."

Bud surreptitiously slipped his revolver out of his pocket and passed it to Paddy under the table. The bobby walked toward him, pointed his baton at Bud, and ordered him to stand up. He eased himself out of his chair.

"Were you just in Rose's Tavern, around the corner?" he asked.

Paddy interrupted. "He's been in here with us all afternoon."

"Quiet!" the bobby shouted. "I'm not talking to you now, am I?" He faced Bud again. "Were you just in Rose's?"

"No, sir."

"Get up and walk a few steps for me, Sergeant."

"Why?"

"Just do it," the man snapped.

Bud stood and took three steps toward the bar and returned, trying with all his might to disguise his limp.

The other policeman then held out his hand. "Hand over your gun."

Bud lifted both hands. "I'm unarmed, sir."

The second officer stepped closer, stuck his face in front of him, and ran his free hand down Bud's pockets, front and back. "He's clean." He sounded disappointed. He looked over at the rest of the men. "But we don't want any trouble from you Sinn Fein boys."

"I'm not lookin' for trouble, Officer," Bud said.

"Good. Are you from around here, Sergeant?"

"No. I'm only here in Dover visitin' relatives, and I came to the pub with my mates here to enjoy a pint. I'm leavin' soon to go home to Ireland."

"Well, don't stay here too long," the officer growled. Both men turned to leave, and when Bud snapped a salute at their backs, some men in the crowd chuckled. One policeman spun around, and the chuckling stopped. He gave Bud a long look, then stalked out with his partner.

The piano player started up again, and the men at the bar resumed their conversations. Bud sat down as Paddy returned the Bulldog, which he slipped back into his pocket.

"What are you playin' at, mate?" Paddy inquired with a frown. "Why are the police lookin' for you?"

Bud sighed. "I stepped into Rose's Tavern to have a beer,

and some English blokes were lookin' to start up with me. I pulled my pistol on them, and that was the end of the trouble. No one got hurt."

"How do you feel about the damned English?" Paddy pursued.

"I feel no particular loyalty to the British. I volunteered to fight in their army to protect Ireland."

Paddy snorted. "Hell, mate, the English have been in Ireland for eight hundred years. We're thinkin' it's time they left."

Bud stood up. "Look at this uniform, Paddy. I'm a British soldier, for God's sake. I can't tell the Brits what to do."

Paddy nodded. "Come back tomorrow night, Sarge. There's someone I think you should meet. And don't wear that damned uniform. It makes people here at McGinty's nervous."

* * *

The next day, Bud again signed out of the rehab center and used some of his back pay to buy some civilian clothes. That evening he limped over to McGinty's, where he found Paddy and the other two men at the back table. He signaled the bartender to pour a round on him, then joined them.

"Who is this man you want me to meet, Paddy?"

"He'll turn up in a few minutes. He's with Sinn Fein, and he used to be with the Irish Volunteers in Westport. Now he's with the Irish Republican Army. He recruits soldiers to join the cause."

Bud stiffened. He wasn't about to be recruited. He'd had enough of fighting.

"His name's Billy Egan," Paddy continued. "He's on the run. The Brits want him for sedition."

"I've no great love for the English," Bud said slowly, "but I'm not sure about the IRA."

"The revolution has already started," Paddy said. "Ireland needs its own republic. We want to be free from England."

At that moment a short, balding man in dusty trousers and a wrinkled shirt made his way to the back of the room and without a word sat down at the table with them. Paddy ordered him a beer.

"I'm Billy Egan," the man said. "I understand you're Emerson Ryan."

"Good to meet you, Billy. Call me Bud. I hear you stand with the IRA."

"And a Republican I am," Billy responded. "We're lookin' for fighting men to help free Ireland from the Brits. We need men like you, men with military training."

"No," Bud announced. "Not me."

"Paddy tells me you're from Westport. We have a strong group in Westport, and we could use your help. Have you heard of Joe Ring?"

"No," Bud said again.

"He's the commander of the Westport Flying Column. They operate in western County Mayo in and around Westport. Can I set up a meetin'?"

Bud hesitated. "I don't think so. I'm not right for the Column. All I know is trench warfare, hundreds of thousands of soldiers fightin' hundreds of thousands of soldiers. None of that is goin' on in Ireland. I'd need to think this over."

Two new patrons entered the pub, and Billy cut off the conversation. He studied them and finally shifted his eyes away. "How long have you been in the British Army, Bud?"

The question made him vaguely uneasy. "Four years, why?"

"Things have changed in Westport since you've been away," Paddy intoned.

At that moment two British bobbies walked in. Toby got up, loudly scraping his chair, and moved past the bar to intercept the police officers. Billy bent toward Bud. "Be here tomorrow," he whispered. "Same time." Then he silently slipped into the shadows and out the back while Toby distracted the police.

Bud and the other two men watched the two bobbies disengage with Toby and work their way back to the table where they sat. They stared hard at all of them. "We're looking for Billy Egan. Any of you micks know him?"

Toby slid back into his seat. "I don't know any Billy Egan. How about you, mates?"

The other two shrugged, and Bud stuffed down a zing of apprehension. Billy Egan was wanted by the British police. As a British soldier, if he got caught with Billy, he could be charged with treason and shot.

That night he thought about both his headstrong brothers, Kevin and Mike. They were members of Sinn Fein, and before he'd enlisted, they had talked about joining the Irish Volunteers. At the time, Bud thought it was all talk. Now he wondered if they'd joined the IRA. Did they know Joe Ring? That thought made him more nervous than evading British bobbies in an Irish pub.

Then his thoughts turned to Rose, waiting for him at home. God, he ached to be with her again. He didn't want to join any fighting group; he wanted to marry Rose and live in peace.

The next morning, he asked a nurse for writing paper and a pen. He knew he had to be careful what he wrote because of the military censors, and he suspected letters addressed anywhere in Ireland would be looked at closely. So, he'd be careful. He picked up the pen.

Dearest Rose,

I'm getting better fast and I can't stand not being with you. I see you in my dreams, and I want to hold you in my arms and never let go. They're going to release me next week, and that means I should be home Saturday the 27ᵗʰ around seven in the evening. Just in time for the pilgrimage to Craugh Patrick, if you remember how that was for us. Please meet me at the Westport train depot. I can't wait to see you.

All my love,

Bud

He addressed the envelope to Rose's farm in Murrisk and handed it to the nurse, who glanced at the address and smiled. "Where's Murrisk?" she asked.

"It's a little village five miles outside Westport, in County Mayo. It's at the foot of Craugh Patrick. That's where legend says Saint Patrick drove the snakes out of Ireland."

She grinned. "I'll get this in the mail right away."

Chapter Three

Going Home

A week later Bud was finally discharged from the rehab center and given his back pay. He decided to wear his uniform on the two-hour train ride to London, which was mostly through the industrial cities of southern England with a short segment through the English countryside. In London he changed trains for Liverpool.

During the six-hour train ride, he encountered a trio of soldiers in British uniforms, a corporal and two privates. All wore the orange unit patch of the 36th Ulster Division. Orange indicated they were Protestants, but Bud overcame his initial feelings of distrust and decided to be friendly. He stood up and moved over to their side of the car.

"Hello, mates. Headin' home?"

The three men looked up at him skeptically. "We are, to be sure," one said. "I didn't know you Sinn Fein boys were friendly with Ulstermen."

Bud took an empty seat. "I served at the Somme, in the trenches, defendin' Ronssoy."

"The three of us were on your flank, Sarge."

He nodded. "The Jerries launched their spring offensive right over our position, and I got shot in the hip and breathed a little mustard gas. Woke up at a French aid station, and they told me your division had launched a counterattack. They also said a couple of your men picked me up and brought me in. So, I owe my life to you Ulstermen."

The men visibly relaxed. For the next hour Bud sat with them, trading war stories, until the train arrived at Liverpool. As they disembarked, they all shook hands. "Good luck to ya, mick," the corporal said.

Bud flinched. The man's tone was friendly enough, but there it was--even after sharing a battlefield and his confession of his debt to Ulstermen, to them he was just another 'mick'.

He caught a cab to a cheap traveler's hotel near the docks, and when he arrived, he inhaled a deep breath of the salty sea air blowing in off Liverpool Bay. A fit of coughing caught him by surprise, and he realized his damaged lungs still hurt.

He spent a restless night thinking about his homeland. And Rose. He could hardly wait to see them again. In the morning, he changed into civilian clothes and caught the Dublin ferry. The ride seemed to take forever, and at the first sight of land, a thrill went through him. He'd not seen Ireland in four long years.

He shook off the memory of battlefields and trenches and limped off the ferry and smiled to himself thinking about Rose waiting for him at the Westport depot. All at once he wondered if his limp and injured lungs would affect her feelings for him.

He boarded a crowded train for Westport and took a window seat. Another man sat down next to him, but Bud angled his body away. At this moment he wanted to be left alone, so he looked out at the land, watching the grass-covered hills, grazing cows, and sheep. He couldn't help thinking about Rose, but he found himself growing nervous about seeing her. Would she notice his limp? Would it matter?

When the train pulled into the Westport station, he fought his way off the platform and into the crowded terminal, then craned his neck, looking for Rose's copper-colored hair.

He didn't see her. Deflated, he turned back toward the

entrance, then spied his older brother, Kevin. Mike was with him. Both of them looked thinner. Kevin opened his arms wide and hugged him until he couldn't breathe. "Welcome home, Bud." He pounded Bud's back with tears in his eyes. "Rose told us you'd been wounded. Are you all right?"

"Ahh, just got nipped," he said when he could breathe. "Got me sent home, though, so it was worth it." He stopped and searched the terminal again. "I don't see Rose. Where is she?"

Kevin and Mike looked at each other. "She's in quarantine."

"Quarantine! Is she sick?"

"Calm yourself," Kevin said. "Her brother Phil's got the Spanish flu, so the whole family's in quarantine. Nobody else in the family is sick, but Dr. Reilly's worried about all the people comin' to Westport for Reek Sunday and the pilgrimage up Craugh Patrick. He doesn't want this flu spreading all over Ireland."

Bud shook his head. "But we have flu outbreaks every year."

"Not like this," Mike said heavily. "This strain is deadly. They call it the black flu because the victims turn purple and then black before they die."

A cold hand closed around Bud's heart. "I don't care about a quarantine. I've waited four years to see Rose."

42

Kevin took him by the arm. "Well, not today, boyo. They're sayin' the flu came over from France, so Dr. Reilly wants us to keep you away from everyone for a week to make sure you're not bringin' the sickness home.

Bud shook his head. "I was at the rehab center in Dover for months. No one there's sick with the flu."

"Sorry, Bud. That's what Dr. Reilly is sayin', and Constable Milling is backin' him up. Give it a week and you're clear."

"A week! I can't wait a week to see Rose!"

"Looks like you've got no choice, Bud, so be patient. Besides, we want to get caught up with you, too. What are your plans now that you're home?"

Bud shrugged. "Look for a job, I guess."

"We're givin' you three days to rest and get your feet under you," Kevin said. "If you don't have something goin' by then, we want you to tend bar for us. You know, chat with our customers. Might be somethin' will come from it."

Mike grabbed his duffel bag and pointed to the terminal exit. "So, you're comin' home with us, boyo. Let's go."

They walked out of the station into the gathering darkness and caught a horse-drawn cab. "Ryan Brothers tavern," Kevin yelled at the driver.

The driver snapped his whip, and the giant draft horse clopped slowly along the cobblestone street toward Westport's Catholic neighborhood. Bud leaned back in his seat and released a long breath.

"Sure, is good to be back. You don't realize how much you miss home until you're gone."

They left the market section of the city just as a street worker was lighting the gaslights. Everything looked the same. The two-story buildings had been built at different times by different builders, but they all touched each other. As they passed into the rougher, Catholic section, the apartment houses and homes were also two-story, but a narrow sidewalk ran between the buildings.

Bud told his brothers what it had been like in France and the things he'd seen during the war. He added that while France was a Catholic country, there was obvious affluence everywhere. Whenever the conversation lapsed, Bud's thoughts returned to Rose. He was disappointed that she wasn't at the station to meet him, but now he was worried about her and the quarantine. *What if she catches this flu? Could I lose her?*

They arrived at Ryan Brothers tavern on the corner of Channel and Island roads at the edge of Westport, and Bud swallowed. He hadn't realized how much he'd missed this place.

Kevin paid the cabbie, and Bud picked up his bag, then stopped to study his old home. "You put a new coat of paint on this old building," he commented.

"Yeah, it needed it," Mike said. "We did the job ourselves, with some help from friends. Your room's still the same. We kept it that way on purpose."

Inside, while Kevin and Mike served the patrons in the tavern, Bud climbed the stairs to the living quarters. His tiny room was just as he remembered it, a narrow single bed covered with a hand-made quilt and a three-drawer dresser with a bare top. No pictures on the wall. He opened the small closet to find it empty. He glanced down the hallway to the master bedroom, commandeered by Kevin after their parents were killed in the bar massacre. They had died the same day Home Rule was enacted, when an argument erupted between Protestants and Republicans, and guns came out. Both their mother and father had died in the crossfire.

He closed his bedroom door and looked out the window into the moonlit backyard, and there he saw exactly what he wanted to see. Inside that old wooden shed, he knew his rusty blue bicycle hung on hooks under the roof. He waited until full dark and the rest of the household had quieted, then eased the window open and climbed down the gutter spout.

The night was warm and muggy, typical for a late July evening. Quietly he walked his bicycle through the back gate, then pedaled the five miles south to Murrisk and turned onto the country lane that led to Rose Ludden's farm. At the back of the yard, bordered by a rock wall fence, stood the two-story thatched farmhouse with the whitewashed plaster walls and a wisp of grey smoke coming from the chimney. The hay barn and two small outbuildings were thatched and whitewashed to match the main house.

It was well past ten o'clock and he was beginning to realize how tired he was. Nevertheless, he leaned his bicycle against the house and tapped at the front door.

Rose opened the door. Maggie was peering over her shoulder, and he was startled to see that both of them wore gauze masks. He didn't wait for Rose to say anything, just stepped in close and wrapped his arms around her. Then he lifted her off the ground, pulled her mask down, and kissed her.

He held her until he could speak, but when words failed him, he kissed her again. Finally, she broke their embrace. "Bud! Oh, Bud." She started to cry. "I'm so glad you've come, but you shouldn't have. You shouldn't have kissed me because we have the flu here, and I don't want you to catch it. I didn't think you could come because of the quarantine."

He looked down at the familiar sprinkle of freckles over her nose and cheeks as she pulled the mask up. "It's been four years, Rose. Nothing could keep me away. I know Phil has the black flu, but could you come away with me anyway?"

Maggie interrupted. "Rose can't leave, Bud. She's needed here."

Bud stared at the tall woman standing in the doorway. "You're in more danger than I am. You could both catch this flu."

"We've both already been exposed, Bud," Rose said quickly. "That's why we're all quarantined and wearin' these masks. We've both been sick and we recovered. Dr. Reilly says we had a light case, but he wants us to wear these masks anyway."

"And then there's Phil," Maggie reminded.

"Yes," Rose breathed. "I know. I need to be here to help take care of Phil."

At that moment headlights lit up the road, and a black Ford rolled to a stop outside the rock fence. The car lights winked out, and Kevin and Mike climbed out. "We didn't figure you'd stay in the house," Kevin yelled. "When we found your room empty it wasn't hard to figure out where you'd gone."

Mike dropped Bud's duffel bag at the gate. "Now you're stuck here for a week."

"Are you kidding? Where am I goin' to sleep?"

Kevin shrugged. "Shoulda thought of that before, boyo." He grinned at Rose, then climbed back into the car with Mike, waved once, and drove off.

Bud stared at the receding taillights. In a way he was

glad his brothers had left him here. He had a million things he wanted to say to Rose. But all at once he realized something.

"I can't stay here, Rose. You've got sickness in the house, and you don't have room for an extra person."

"You could sleep in the hay barn," she suggested.

"The barn?" Bud spun to look at the huge structure. "Well, sure. Compared to where I've been sleepin' for the last four years, your barn looks like Buckingham Palace." He retrieved his duffel and dropped it inside the barn door.

Rose and Maggie disappeared back into the house, and Bud climbed up into the loft. At least he was warm and dry and he would be only a hundred feet away from Rose. Better than a few thousand miles with machine guns and sniper fire for company.

A few minutes later, Rose appeared with a bowl of shepherd's stew and a glass of homemade mead, a Ludden family specialty. She reached into her skirt pocket and produced two lumps of what looked like cloudy, yellow candy.

"What's this?"

"They're lozenges made from formaldehyde and lactose. Mrs. O'Neil says they help ward off the plague."

He bent his head and sniffed. "They smell awful."

"Just suck on them after you finish eating. The other

thing we've been using is whiskey and ginger. I'll bring some out later. It's not too bad; in fact, I've grown to like it." She paused as if uncertain what to say next. Then she looked up at him. "I'll see you later," she said softly.

He wolfed down the shepherd's stew and tried one of the lozenges but spit it out. He spit again to get the taste out of his mouth. *What I really need is that whiskey. Oh, hell, what I really need is Rose.*

When he could no longer keep his eyes open, he made himself a nest in the hay, stretched out, and closed his eyes. It all seemed unreal, coming home. He thought he might be dreaming until he heard a noise below and glimpsed Rose's red hair in the moonlight.

She climbed the ladder up to the loft, balancing a tall glass of whiskey and ginger. Bud put the concoction down next to him, slipped her mask down, and pulled her close. His head began to swim as he kissed her. God, he wanted her so much, but he knew now was not the time.

"I want to stay here with you tonight," Rose whispered. "I'll have to go back to the house before the sun comes up, but there's so much to say. Besides, I don't want you to be alone on your first night home."

They talked until past midnight and shared the whiskey and ginger. Much later, when Rose nestled beside him, Bud heard an odd sound, like a fox keening. Instantly he remembered the legend of the banshee and a shiver went up his spine.

Hours later, he heard a woman's voice. "Rose, are you up there?"

Rose sat up. "Yes, Maggie. What is it?"

"It's Phil. You need to go into Westport and get Father Blaney."

Rose stood and brushed straw from her dress. "You mean Dr. Reilly?"

"No," Maggie said in a shaky voice. "Phil is beyond what Dr. Reilly can do. I think he needs Last Rites."

Rose sucked in her breath and started to cry.

"I'll go," Bud volunteered. He kissed Rose, then scrambled down the ladder, mounted his bicycle, and pedaled hard for Westport.

Joe Ring

Chapter Four

Honoring Phil Ludden

There would be no wake for Phil Ludden. Dr. Reilly forbid it. While the family planned a memorial service, Bud was asked to make arrangements for Phil's burial. There would also be no funeral Mass. Only a 15-minute memorial service would be allowed, and that had to wait a week while the family was cleared of any infection. After Rose and Maggie disinfected Phil's room, Bud moved into the house.

The memorial service was planned for St. Mary's Church in Westport, with Father Blaney officiating. Before the ceremony, Rose took Bud aside. "I should warn you there might be trouble at the memorial."

"Trouble? What kind of trouble?"

Rose sighed. "The service will be attended by mostly Republican sympathizers. Our whole family stands with the resistance to British rule, and Constable Milling knows this. I just hope he stays away and lets us be."

The service began at ten. The church was already crowded with family members and friends when a tall, good-looking young man arrived with two other men about the same age. He was clearly a celebrity, as his presence seemed to fill the room, and everyone wanted to shake his hand. Standing at the front, Bud leaned over to Rose. "Who is that?" he murmured.

"That's Joe Ring," she responded in a hushed voice. "And those are his brothers, Jack and Walter."

Joe Ring came over to speak with Rose's grieving mother and father, and Bud asked Rose to introduce him.

She led him to the line of people waiting to talk with Ring and his brothers, and when it came their turn, Joe stepped forward and embraced Rose. "Phil was a good man," he said quietly. "One of the best."

Rose introduced Bud to Joe, then to his brothers, Jack and Walter. Maggie then interrupted conversation to steer Walter outside, and the rest of the mourners moved on into the parlor.

"Rose, tell me about this man, Joe Ring."

Rose pulled him into a corner and spoke quickly. "His

full name is Michael Joseph Ring, named for his father. A few years ago, Joe was trainin' some Irish Volunteers out in the country and Constable Milling showed up with some deputies and arrested him. Milling said he wanted to make an example of the leader. They charged Joe with sedition, sentenced him to six months hard labor, and sent him to Frongoch prison in Wales. While he was there, he met Michael Collins and some other Sinn Fein leaders. I think that all the prison time did was unite Sinn Fein across Ireland."

"What about the brothers?" Bud asked.

Walter is Maggie's fiancé. Jack is Joe's right-hand man, and they all stand for Irish independence."

"Why are they here? Did they know Phil?"

Rose hesitated. "Phil was a member of Sinn Fein. Anyone at this memorial service will be suspected of being Sinn Fein."

Later, at the church, Father Blaney stood at the communion railing and lifted his hands, signaling the congregation to quiet down. Then he invited anyone who wanted to speak about Phil Ludden to come forward. After a pause, Joe Ring rose and stepped to the front of the congregation.

"I have known Phil Ludden most of me life," he said, his voice quiet. "I can tell you that he was a real patriot. He was dedicated to liberatin' Ireland, and that's because for eight hundred years the English have ruled over us. They rule, and yet they allow us no voice at all. It is sad that Phil, who believed in Irish independence, won't be able to enjoy the fruits of our struggle."

He paused and studied the mourners. "Like many of us, Phil believed that we need a republic of our own. He believed we have to take Ireland back from the English."

A murmur ran through the congregation, and after a moment Joe went on. "Not too long ago our friends in Dublin made a stand on Easter Sunday, and you all know what happened on that day. British soldiers arrested them and put them in prison. Then they took them out, all fourteen of them, and shot them. Phil wasn't the only one of us to be shocked and saddened by what the British did that day. All Ireland mourned."

At this, Joe paused for effect, and the mourners began to stir restlessly. "Now Phil is gone, but we can't let his spirit die, and we can't let his hopes for the Irish republic wither away. Phil Ludden would want all of you to join with us in resisting the Eng ..."

Suddenly the church doors at the back of the church banged open, and Constable John Milling, in full uniform, appeared. He surveyed the mourners, then pulled a small notebook from his pocket and began to write.

"Constable Milling," Joe called in a ringing voice, "you are not welcome here. We are buryin' our dead and want to be left in peace."

Some of the younger men began to edge their way out of the pews, but Ring stopped them with a look. Then he marched down the aisle toward the constable. "This is a private memorial service, Constable, and it's none of your concern. I'm askin' you to please leave." He stopped halfway to the door, swept his hand toward the mourners and said in a polite tone, "Gentlemen, please see Constable Milling to the door."

Eight men scrambled from their seats. Bud rose to follow and felt a rush of adrenalin.

Constable Milling inched backwards. The first man to reach him tore the notebook out of his hand. Two others spun him around and shoved him out the door. Bud followed them outside where two uniformed deputy constables were leaning against a black patrol car.

They straightened when Milling stumbled through the church door toward them, followed by some of the mourners. The deputies drew their batons and moved forward, and by then Bud's adrenaline was pumping. He felt for his revolver and limped down the church steps to join the melee when a voice shouted from behind him, and he pulled up short.

Father Blaney stood at the top of the steps. "Stop this!" the priest shouted. "There will be no violence on this holy ground!"

Joe Ring joined him. "Constable Milling," he called, "we ask you to leave this place of worship and take your deputies with you."

The men of the congregation surrounded the constables, and tempers began to flare. The deputies shoved the mourners, and the mourners pushed back, but no punches were thrown. Bud's heart pounded with relief.

"This isn't finished, Ring," the constable yelled.

"Would you be tryin' to start a riot?" Ring asked calmly. "Leave us to bury our dead in peace."

Milling shot him a black look. Then he and his deputies climbed back in their car and roared off. Joe Ring watched them as the congregation drifted back to the church, and then once again he took his place at the communion railing. "We are here to honor Phil Ludden and his patriotic spirit," he said slowly. "May he rest in peace."

When Phil Ludden was properly remembered and the service concluded, Bud talked with Rose for a long time, then caught a ride back to the tavern with Kevin.

"Will you be comin' to the Sinn Fein meetin' tomorrow?" Kevin wanted to know. "We're finally goin' to take some action."

"What kind of action?"

"I don't know. Joe Ring has something cooked up for Sinn Fein to do."

Bud hesitated. *Sinn Fein?* Am I going to jump from the frying pan right into the fire? Everyone around here is angry, but I guess going to a meeting wouldn't be too risky. I should at least know what's going on.

"Where's this meetin' to be?"

"We don't know yet. Joe changes the location every time. A car will pick us up about half-past five. Sometimes these meetings are out on the glen, at an abandoned building somewhere, so dress warm. Sometimes they go on until late. And Bud, you should come armed with that little pistol you carry."

Come armed? What in God's name was he getting into?

That afternoon around five, Bud pulled on a heavy sweater and slipped his revolver into his pocket. A few minutes later, a black Renault pulled up with tall, blond Joe Gill behind the wheel and Rick Mills in the front seat next to him. Rick was short and thick-set, but he moved like an athlete. His close-cropped hair was dark red. Bud hadn't seen either of them since he'd been sent to France. He climbed into the back seat with Kevin and Mike, and Gill drove 30 minutes north of Westport, then pulled up behind a car that was stopped next to a rail fence. Three men were gathered around it, apparently fixing the front tire.

Joe Gill climbed out of the Renault. "What are you men doin' out here?"

No answer. But all four men began studying the deserted road. Finally, Gill jogged back to the Renault. "It's all clear," he whispered. "We're the last ones."

One of the three jumped on the running board while another removed a rail from the fence. After they drove through, two of the men resumed supposedly fixing the tire. Bud noticed a shotgun leaning up against the car, out of sight of the road.

The fellow on the running board directed the Renault through the pasture and around a hill on a rough path hidden from the road. They ended up at an old, abandoned farmhouse with a thatched roof. Carriage horses were tied to a rail fence where two saddled horses were tethered. A guard cradling a shotgun walked up and down in front of the house.

The front door was low, so low they had to stoop to enter. Inside it looked like an abandoned version of the Ludden home, but here the floors were filthy, the few windows lacked glass panes, and the place smelled of mildew. A jumble of wooden chairs spread over the bare floor, but there were no tables or other furniture. The windows didn't block the wind from the outside, and it was cold.

Bud dusted off a chair and took a seat, and after a few minutes Joe Ring stood up. "Looks like everyone is here. Gentlemen, I'd like you to meet a new member of our column, Bud Ryan."

Whoa. Jesus, he hadn't decided to join Joe Ring's group. Still, Bud half-rose and nodded at the others.

Joe then cleared his throat. "What's on the table tonight is makin' an actual raid on British authority in Westport. I've been sendin' Constable Milling letters warnin' him to get out of Ireland, but he's been ignorin' them. So now I propose that we do somethin' that gets his attention. I proposed that we torch his racin' yacht, which is moored at the Westport Quay."

"Why?" Kevin Ryan asked.

Joe Ring studied him for a moment. "We need to strike at the Brits' strength to get our message across. I say we burn and sink John Milling's yacht. Then he'll know we mean business."

Ring's brother, Jack, spoke up. "Joe, you're obsessed with John Milling. What's so important about a yacht?"

"John Milling represents British authority in Westport," Joe responded. "One thing I learned in prison is that we have to attack English authority wherever and in whatever form it is. John Milling represents British rule in Ireland. He enforces English law, laws in which we Irish have no say."

Bud had to admit Joe Ring had a point there. A very good point. The Irish people *should* have a say in their own government.

"Then," Joe went on, "when the constable makes an arrest, he acts not only as the police but as the judge as well. That's unfair. I say we should have a country ruled by the Irish."

Rick Mills levered his bulk to a standing position. "And just how are we goin' to accomplish this?" he queried.

Ring sent him a withering look. "Well, mates, just listen to my plan."

Chapter Five

The Strike

Joe Ring held the men's attention as he laid out his plan. "We're goin' to need six men for this operation. First off, we place two armed guards at the land end of the quay. Then four more of us launch a rowboat from the woods opposite the seaside end of the concrete dock. We tie the boat up on the sea end, and someone stays with it. I'll lead the other three men down the pier to Milling's yacht, and we'll pepper it with glass bottles filled with gasoline."

Bud closed his eyes. *Christ above, man, that's sabotage. Fighting for Irish independence should be clean, fought with bullets and bombs, not with gasoline.*

Bud ran his hand through his hair and felt his insides

tighten. *That yacht is expensive. If we get caught, we'll be charged with arson and then with sedition, plain and simple. For what? To scare the constable?*

"Then," Joe continued, "we run back down the quay, get in the boat, and row like hell for the woods. When our guards on the other end see the flames, they just melt away in the opposite direction."

Bud studied his hands. *I can't believe I spent four years in the trenches in France, up to my hips in blood and gore, friends dying in my arms, only to come home and listen to adults talk about breaking each other's toys. This is insane.*

He took a deep breath. "That won't do it," he heard himself say. "If you're really goin' to do somethin' this daft, the bottles need to be thrown inside the yacht, below deck, not on the top. That would conceal the flames a little longer and give the three men time to get back to the boat and into the woods without being seen. It also guarantees more damage."

"He's right," someone commented.

Bud swallowed. "If the bottles are just tossed on the top deck, someone on shore might see the flames and have time to put the fire out."

"Good point," Ring said. "I'll change the plan."

Rick Mills spoke up again. "Whose rowboat are we goin' to use?"

"We have to steal one," Joe said. "If we borrow one from a mate and it's discovered, the owner would be in trouble. Anyway, I've already stolen a deputy constable's rowboat. It's hidden in the woods opposite the quay."

"When are we goin' to do this?" Joe Walsh asked. Walsh was too chubby to have ever rowed a boat anywhere, Bud thought. So, what did his 'we' mean?

"The day after tomorrow is a new moon, the darkest night of the month," Ring said. "I say we hit them then, about two in the morning. The streets will be deserted. Bud and Kevin Ryan can guard the land end of the quay. If anybody's wanderin' around there, you just delay and distract them. Bring guns you can conceal, but try not to use them."

Bud stared at him. *Ring is serious about this. He's got this all worked out. So, Sergeant Ryan, now that you've been invited to the party, what are you gonna do?*

Ring glanced at the men and seemed to read their minds. "Look mates, burnin' this man's toy doesn't sound like much, but Constable Milling has ignored months of warnin's to leave Ireland. We need to take an action that clearly warns him without hurtin' anybody. All he loses is his yacht, but he can't ignore this kind of warnin'."

Bud made his decision. *All right, I'm for Irish independence, so I guess that means I'm going to burn up*

Constable Milling's yacht. In for a penny, in for a pound.

Ring returned to the details of the plan, and Bud listened to another hour of discussion with a feeling of wary commitment until the meeting was finally over. He and Kevin got back in the Renault with the men who had brought them. The rest of the men climbed into carriages or mounted their horses. With Joe Ring's carriage in the lead, they all made their way back toward the hill that obscured the abandoned farmhouse. When they sighted the road, Ring leaned out and signaled the two men who were still pretending to fix a flat tire. One removed the fence rail, and all the men drove out onto the road and disappeared in opposite directions.

Once headed for home, Bud turned to Kevin. "Is this what Sinn Fein is all about? Torchin' yachts?"

Kevin didn't answer. Bud spent the rest of the trip home wondering why Joe said to bring weapons if they weren't going to hurt anybody.

That night he had another one of his nightmares. He heard the voices of thousands of screaming German soldiers coming at him. He fired his rifle until it was empty, but none of them stopped, they kept coming. Then he fired his Bulldog until he ran out of ammunition, but still the Germans just kept coming. He tried to run, but he found he couldn't move. German soldiers surrounded him, and thrust their bayonets into his body, over and over. He kept shouting, "Stop! Stop! *Stop!*" But they didn't stop.

Someone shook him, and then he heard Kevin's voice. "Bud! *Bud!* Wake up. What's wrong?"

Bud sat up and wiped his forehead with a shaking hand.

"I could hear you yellin' from downstairs. Are you all right?"

He pulled his sweat-soaked pajamas away from his chest. "Guess I was havin' a nightmare. I'm okay, Kevin. Go on back downstairs."

"Are you sure?"

No, he wasn't sure. But Kevin didn't need to know that. At the rehab center they'd given him sleeping pills, but here at home he had nothing to take for the nightmares. He stared up at the ceiling and tried to calm his hammering heart.

He needed to get his life back to normal, find a job. He'd go looking in the morning, he decided. Later maybe he'd cycle out to see Rose and try not to think about tomorrow night and Constable Milling's yacht.

* * *

He woke up early and pulled on his good trousers and a clean shirt, then pedaled his bicycle down Westport's business street. He stopped in at carpentry shops and automotive guilds, even grocery stores and newsstands. It wasn't encouraging. Recruiters kept calling him "mick," and though he walked his bike up and down the entire business section, he found nothing. At three that afternoon, he returned to Ryan Brothers tavern to begin his shift at the bar. There were lots of customers, and when he got a conversation going, he'd always ask about jobs. He finally got used to them shaking their heads.

Around five, Rose walked in and leaned over the bar to plant a kiss on his cheek.

"What are you doin' in town?" he asked.

"Shoppin'. I know you're off tomorrow, Bud. Are you comin' over?"

"I can come for supper, but I'm ... um ... meetin' some friends later on. Would you have a little time now?"

"Sure."

He shouted down the bar, "Kevin, I'm takin' a break. Can you cover?"

"Go ahead." Kevin grinned and waved. "Hi, Rose."

Bud steered her to a quiet table at the back of the tavern. "Are you hungry?"

"I could handle a sandwich."

He ducked into the kitchen and reappeared with two cheese sandwiches and two glasses of milk. He sat down next to her and kissed her.

She pulled away. "Somethin's botherin' you, Bud. What is it?"

"I'm not havin' much luck findin' a job."

"Have you thought about rentin' a small farm? There are plenty around now that so many people have given up and gone to America."

"No. Farmin's not for me." Then, he leaned close to her and whispered, "There's somethin' else."

"What?" she murmured.

"We're makin' a move against Constable Milling. Tonight."

She stared at him, her eyes widening. "What do you mean? Who is 'we'?"

"Sinn Fein. We're goin' to torch his yacht down at the quay."

"What time?"

Bud frowned. "Two in the mornin'. Why is that important?"

"I'm comin' with you."

He jolted upright and shook his head. "Oh, no, you're not. There could be trouble, and I don't want you involved."

"Maggie and I used to go with Phil for trainin' with Joe Ring. We learned some nursin' skills and got some practice with guns. The idea was that we could care for anyone who got injured, and we could also act as lookouts."

"Yeah," he said. "Good for you and Maggie. But this—"

"I want to come, Bud. I'll be here by midnight."

He gritted his teeth. He admired Rose's courage, but he'd be carrying a gun. It could be dangerous. "You're not goin'," he said.

She set her jaw. "I'm comin', Bud Ryan, and that's all there is to it."

"You're not goin'," he said again.

She reached out and shook his forearm. "What is the plan?"

He told her what they were going to do and explained his part in it.

"It would be easier if you had a woman on your arm when you're guardin' the quay. I'm comin' with you."

He gave her a long look. The determined set of her jaw told him she wasn't going to back down, so he finally nodded. He leaned over and kissed her cheek. "Be here at midnight."

"Midnight," she breathed. She rested her hand on his thigh. "Anythin' to spend some more time with you."

Margaret Ludden Ring

* * *

After another fruitless day spent looking for work, Bud again ended up behind the bar serving the customers. He told Kevin that Rose was coming along that night and was surprised when his brother didn't object.

As the sun set, a cold wind came up. At midnight, as the bar emptied, Rose showed up with Maggie, both wearing heavy coats and knitted hats.

"Why is Maggie here?" Bud hissed.

"She's comin' with us. She's goin' to pose as Kevin's girl. That's how we're goin' to do this, as double dates walkin' down by the quay."

"I don't know if Joe's goin' to go along with this. Good planners don't like surprises."

"Tell him we just improved his plan."

"Rose, I don't have a good feelin' about this. I don't want you and Maggie in the middle of it if somethin' goes wrong."

She propped her hands on her hips. "Too late. We're already here, and we're goin' with you."

After the tavern emptied, Bud went up to his room and pulled on an extra sweater and a heavy jacket. Kevin locked up the bar, and all of them stepped outside. The wind was up, and Bud could smell rain coming. He didn't want Rose and Maggie along, and he prayed this would end safely. Not for the first time was he wondering what Maggie was about. And Rose … Good God, he couldn't believe how calm she looked. Apparently, the Ludden sisters had nerves of steel. Sure hoped that was true of the Ryan brothers tonight.

It was a mile and a half to the quay, and with every step he could feel Rose's hand tighten in his. They took up stations near the entrance to the quay, next to the boatmaster's hut. A quick look inside told him it was empty, and they ambled along to study the other buildings. All were deserted at this time of night, and it was so dark they couldn't see down the concrete pier until a bolt of lightning backlit the quay. There was no sign of Joe Ring and the rest of the men.

The wind picked up as the rainstorm blew in toward shore. Just as Kevin bent to light a cigarette, a voice suddenly boomed from behind them. "Hey, what are you doing out here?"

Two patrolmen approached. One was as tall as Bud, the other considerably shorter.

"Just enjoyin' a walk after work," Bud responded easily.

Kevin stepped toward the men. "What are *you* doin' here?"

"Just … patrollin', like always."

Out of the corner of his eye Bud saw Rose pull

something out of her coat pocket. My God, it was a gun! Instantly, he pushed her hand back down. She took the hint and slowly slid the weapon out of sight. Neither of the two men noticed.

"Nice night for a walk," Kevin said with a laugh. "This wind keeps our girls close, it does."

After some more banter, the two men walked off toward the business district, and Bud breathed a sigh of relief.

Another bolt of lightning lit up the pier, and he glimpsed four dark figures gliding up in a rowboat. It thumped up against the concrete, and Bud swiveled his head in that direction. Another flash of lightning. No thunder, so he figured the storm was still out at sea.

Three men in dark clothing moved in a crouch among the moored boats. One of the men stumbled in the dark, and when he fell, Bud heard the sound of breaking glass.

Jesus, they broke a gasoline bottle.

Rose turned to him and pulled his head down. "What are they goin' to do now, without the gasoline?" she whispered.

He shrugged. "I don't know." In the dark he couldn't see what was going on, but all of a sudden, another bottle shattered, followed a few seconds later by a swoosh of flames as someone on the yacht tossed a match. Another bottle broke against the yacht's hull, and the flames leaped higher.

In the firelight Bud could see three men running down the pier toward the rowboat.

The two patrolmen raced toward them. "Hey, what was that?" one yelled. Just as they ran up, the first drops of rain fell.

"Did you see that?" one shouted. By now, flames were consuming the yacht. The other man noticed movement on the quay. "You men! Get back here."

Too late. The three men in the rowboat were pulling hard toward shore. Lightning cracked, followed by a clap of thunder. The larger of the two patrolmen spun toward Bud. "Hey, they're trying to land over there in those woods. Let's go get them!"

"No!" Bud yelled. "Stay here and help me put out this fire."

He used his elbow to smash the window in the boatmaster's hut door, then carefully reached in and unlocked it. Inside, he found four empty red fire brigade buckets stacked in a corner, and he passed them out to Kevin and the two patrolmen. Bud filled his bucket full of bay water, but the flames were too intense to get anywhere near the burning yacht. He edged sideways, covering his face with his bent arm, until he could toss his bucket of water.

"Call the fire brigade," he shouted. "Save the other boats." He bent down, untied the yacht in the adjacent slip, and shoved it away from the quay. Kevin worked on the boat in the next slip.

One of the two patrolmen ran to the volunteer fire alarm and banged the metal rod inside the triangle, yelling "Fire! Fire!"

Constable Milling's yacht was burning, but Rose turned and grabbed his arm. "Bud, why are you puttin' out that fire?"

"I'm not puttin' it out. That first bucket of water helped spread the gasoline. But to avoid suspicion we're goin' to have to wait for the fire brigade."

By the time it arrived, Constable Milling's yacht was engulfed in flames. Brigade volunteer Deputy Constable Harris arrived in rubber boots and a nightshirt and questioned everyone, including the two patrolmen. After an hour, he released them all to go home.

Back at the tavern, Bud took Rose aside. "What are you doin' with a gun, Rose?"

"I told you. Maggie and I have been trainin' with Joe Ring. He conducts firearms trainin' for anyone who supports the cause."

"Have you ever used it?"

"N-not yet. We carry them for protection."

He gritted his teeth. "Protection from what? Rose, you're not active in the IRA, are you?"

"I have to go, Bud," she said quickly. "Alan's pickin' us up."

He held her tight. "Rose, you have to be more careful. I can't risk losing you."

"Oh, Bud. I know there's risk, but don't you see? If we want our freedom from the English, we have to fight for it."

He could think of nothing to say to that, so he bundled Rose and her sister off to catch their ride back to Murrisk, climbed upstairs, and fell into bed.

An hour later Kevin shook him awake. "Would you go downstairs? There's a deputy constable here who wants to talk to you."

Chapter Six

The Hidden Room

Bud pulled on his shirt and a pair of trousers and tramped downstairs to see a uniformed policeman waiting for him at the end of the bar. "Are you lookin' for me?"

"I am. I'm Deputy Harris with the constable's office. We met early this mornin' down at the quay, remember? Is there somewhere we can talk?"

Bud led him to a table at the back of the tavern. "What can I do for you?"

"I'm followin' up on the fire at the Westport quay," the deputy began. "You were with Rose and Maggie Ludden, is that right?"

"It is. Rose is my fiancée."

"Are you aware that her brother, Phil Ludden, was a member of the IRA?"

Bud shrugged. "What does that have to do with Rose? Phil Ludden is dead."

"We believe the entire Ludden family supports the IRA. We also think it's odd that the Ludden sisters just happened to be at the quay on the night Constable Milling's yacht was destroyed."

Bud feigned surprise. "That yacht belonged to John Milling? Faith, I didn't know that."

"I'll bet the Ludden sisters did. The fire burned it down to the water."

"That's unfortunate," Bud said. "But the Ludden sisters had nothin' to do with it. They were with my brother Kevin and me last night. We met up with Rose and Maggie after work, and we decided to take a walk before the storm hit."

"I see."

"Sure, and do you think I'm a member of the IRA?"

"Ah, no," the deputy said quickly. "I'm not saying that. Just wanted to know whose idea it was to walk down to the quay on a rainy night."

Bud shifted in his chair. "Sometimes when the girls are in town, they treat us by comin' by the tavern after work. There's no place open at that hour, so we take a walk."

"They wanted to walk in the rain?"

"It wasn't rainin' when we left the tavern."

Deputy Harris rose and extended his hand. "I see I'm making you nervous, Mr. Ryan. Actually, Constable Milling wants to thank you and your brother for saving the yachts that were moored next to his. You did the town a favor." With that, the deputy walked out the tavern door.

In the next moment Bud's brother Mike appeared at his elbow. "What was that all about?"

"They think Rose and Maggie had somethin' to do with destroyin' Constable Milling's yacht last night because they think the whole Ludden family supports the IRA."

"But they do, don't they?" Mike said.

"Yeah, they do all right," Bud said with a sigh. "Even Rose and Maggie. They need to be more careful."

"So last night you burned up Constable Milling's fancy yacht," Mike said with a chuckle. "Joe Ring must be ecstatic. I wonder what he's plannin' next?"

* * *

The following morning Bud headed downstairs to the tavern to sweep up before the first customers arrived. Mike was sitting at a table in the back with his morning mug of tea when Kevin came in, poured himself some tea, and sat down next to him. He invited Bud to join them and then nudged his arm. "I've found a job for you."

Bud sent him a sharp look. "You mean besides servin' drinks and sweepin' up when everyone in the pub is gone?"

Kevin grinned. "We're goin' to renovate the cellar, and part of the deal is that you get to work for the builder."

"What?" Mike exclaimed. "What do you mean, 'renovate the cellar'?"

"It's true," Kevin said. "I just talked to Joe Ring. He got some money, and he's sendin' his builder over to talk about the details."

Mike frowned, leaned forward, and spread his hands on the table. "Kev, what the hell are you talkin' about?"

Kevin looked down at his tea and turned the mug around and around on the table. "You remember when Joe talked to us about buildin' a hiding place in our cellar? You know, a place to stash guns."

"I do remember, but I thought that was all talk." Mike paled and ran his hand through his hair. "Jesus, Kev, what have you done?"

Kevin didn't look up.

Bud looked from one to the other with a sinking feeling in the pit of his stomach. What *had* Kevin done? "What's this all about?"

Kevin leaned back in his chair and studied Mike. "Joe Ring needs a place in town to hide weapons," he explained.

"And maybe ..." He leaned forward. "Maybe someday he might need space for one or two people to hide out. I showed Joe our cellar, and he said he liked it, but a secret room had to be separated off with a wall and a hidden entrance. He didn't say anythin' much after that, so I thought the idea got dropped."

"But it didn't," Bud observed.

Kevin glanced his way. "Nah. Joe said he's received some money from an American member of the Dublin Irish Volunteers, name of Eamon de Valera."

Mike slammed his hand down on the table, and both Kevin and Bud jumped. "I didn't agree to this!" he said loudly. "You realize if we get caught with guns or bombs in our cellar it's prison for all three of us? Or worse," he added. "Kev, how could you make a decision like that without askin' us? Both of us? How could you agree to put us in danger without tellin' us?"

Bud stared at his brothers. "Kevin, don't you think it's just a mite dangerous, hidin' guns right under the nose of the constables? Their station is just down the street."

Kevin, red in the face, leaned in and lowered his voice. "Mike and I have been stuck in this bar our whole lives," he growled. "And there's nothin' better out there as long as the English are runnin' things in Ireland. The bank won't give us a loan to expand this place, even though we showed them the kind of money we make. We won't have opportunities until the English leave. Bud's been lookin' for work, but he can't get hired because they say he's a 'mick'. We're both 'mick's', and that's all there is to it. We have to get the English out of Ireland."

"So?" Mike grumbled.

"So," Kevin continued, "listen to this. A couple of days ago, Sinn Fein won 73 out of 101 seats in the English Parliament. And instead of goin' to Westminster in London, they met in Dublin, declared themselves the First Dail, and proclaimed the Irish Republic. They declared Irish independence! Can you believe this? The English were livid, and right away they voted to outlaw the Dail."

Bud frowned. "Are you kiddin'? That should get things goin'."

"No, I'm not kiddin'," Kevin snapped. "In their first meetin', they elected Cathal Brugha chairman. Brugha was one of the survivors of the 1916 Easter Uprising. I bet now the English wish they'd executed him when they had the chance."

Bud scratched his head. "You mean all seventy-three elected delegates went to Dublin and declared Irish independence?"

"Not all of them. Some of the delegates went to London. They thought formin' the Irish Dail and declarin' the Irish

Republic was goin' too far."

Bud felt a surge of patriotism. Then he wondered how Rose was feeling about this.

"Cripes," Mike said, straightening in his chair. "The English aren't goin' to like that, now are they?"

"Mike, I think Kevin's right," Bud said. "We need to be part of this. Anyway, after days of havin' jobs denied me because I'm a 'mick', at least *I* need to be a part of this."

"Don't you get it, Mike?" Kevin repeated. "We'll be fightin' for Ireland, our *own* Ireland. Joe Ring says his friend Michael Collins is organizin' Flying Columns all over Ireland to drive out the English. Anyway, the least we can do is help Joe Ring out with a hidin' place in our cellar."

"Wait a minute," Bud and Mike said together.

"Yeah? Wait for what?"

"We can't just march blindly into this," Mike said.

"There's no waitin'," Kevin muttered. "There's no waitin'. It's done. And I got Joe to agree that Bud could work with the builder to section off part of our cellar."

"You mean a job?" Bud blurted. "I get paid?"

Kevin playfully punched his arm. "You've got a job. And we get our own country back."

Bud couldn't help grinning. "When do I start?"

"The builder's comin' this afternoon, but this has to be absolutely secret. You can't even tell Rose."

"Just who is this builder?" Mike grumbled.

"Name's Bill."

Mike sighed. "Bill what?"

"That's all, just Bill. The workers aren't from Westport and they don't use their real names. When the job's finished in one place, they move on."

The brothers stared at each other without speaking until Kevin stood up. "Anybody want more tea?"

An hour later, Bill the builder arrived and asked at the bar for Kevin. He was short and well-built, with a red nose and a fringe of red hair. When Kevin told him Bud would be working with him, he pursed his lips. "Got any experience in the trades?"

"I do not," Bud admitted. "I've only been back from the war a few months."

Bill gave him an appraising look. "Well, maybe you can learn somethin'."

Kevin lit an oil lamp and led them all down into the dim cellar. The coal-fired furnace took up most of the room, with vent pipes headed in every direction, and it gave off enough heat to make the cellar pleasantly warm. The coal bin occupied a separate room, and the door between them was left open.

Kevin set the lamp on top of a crate and waved his hand toward the back. "We could get rid of a lot of the stuff stored back there. The rest of the area we use for tavern supplies, but we could move that close to the stairs. That would free up about half the space." He stopped and glanced at Mike. "We won't need the whole front half. The hidden part should be about fifteen feet from the far end. That should give us a pretty large room back there."

Bill nodded. He took out a steel tape, made some measurements, and wrote some notes down on a tablet, then inspected the ceiling and the floor and scratched a few more notes. Finally, he handed Kevin a list.

"It's a simple enough job," Bill said. "Get this end of the cellar cleared out and have the materials on this list delivered by Monday so we can get started."

Bud looked at his two brothers. *When I got back from France, I sure never thought I'd be buildin' a hideout for God knows what.*

Bill started for the stairs. "You'll have to close the tavern for most of one day, from dawn until sometime around six. We'll be makin' a lot of noise down here with hammers and saws, but we'll finish the framin' and anchorin' before you open."

"Right," Kevin intoned.

"We'll need lanterns down here. And we'll bring some blankets to muffle the sound."

They climbed back up to the tavern and shook hands all

around, then Bill walked out the door and disappeared. Kevin handed Bill's list to Bud. "Have everythin' here by Saturday afternoon." Then he reached into his pocket and produced a wad of bills. "This is from Joe Ring. It's only to build the room, so if there's anythin' left over, it goes back to Joe. Use your own money for anythin' else."

Bud nodded and pocketed the bills, and Kevin slapped him on the back. "When you get back from buyin' all this, you need to get the cellar cleaned up, so don't you be pedalin' off to see Rose, now. Joe Ring says he's pressed for time."

Chapter Seven

The Shooting

Before dawn on Monday, someone knocked on the back door of the tavern. Bud heard it, piled out of bed and got dressed, then let 'Rick' and 'Tom' in. He showed them to the cellar and helped them hang up blankets to seal off the work area. When he climbed back up the stairs, the noise of hammering and sawing was barely audible. Mike hung a "Closed Until 6 P.M." sign in the window.

When the framing work was done, Joe Ring arrived, and he, Bill, and Kevin opened the cellar door and tramped downstairs to inspect the renovation project. Joe walked around surveying the area and slowly nodded his head. "Good. Very good."

Bill demonstrated how the spring-loaded hidden panel closed and swung away from the false wall. "This will do very well," Joe said, propping his hands on his hips. "Tomorrow before dawn, my men will start movin' in some guns and ammunition, and I'll also add some medical equipment. Any objections?"

Kevin shook his head.

"And," Joe added, "I'd like to add two cots and a couple of chairs."

When the men walked back upstairs, Bud and the two other builders went back to work. By the time the tavern opened, the hidden cellar room was finished and Joe Ring and Bill the builder had left.

Before sunrise the next morning, a lorry load of rifles, handguns, bayonets, shotguns, explosives, and ammunition was delivered. Watching this, Bud began to feel uneasy. If the constables discovered this hidden cache, his life wouldn't be worth a farthing.

Later that day, two cots, bedding, blankets, and medical equipment appeared.

That evening, as Bud was wiping down the surface of the bar, Kevin walked over. "You comin' tonight?" he asked.

Bud shook out the bar rag and hung it over the sink. "Comin' where?"

"The meetin' at the Ring farm."

He hesitated. "I thought I'd pedal out to see Rose tonight."

"You can see her tomorrow night," Kevin urged. "This is important."

Important, huh? Guess I'd better go out to Ring's farm and see what's up. He nodded at his brother and absentmindedly wet the bar rag again.

At half past midnight, a car pulled up to the back door of the tavern, and Bud, Kevin, and Mike climbed in. The sky was overcast, and a crisp March wind was stirring up the trees. At least it wasn't raining.

When they arrived at the Ring's ramshackle farmhouse, Bud was surprised to see Rose's brothers, Terry and Alan Ludden, already seated next to Jack and Walter Ring. Terry and Alan looked so much alike they could be twins, blond curls and all. Bud noted that Joe Gill, Rick Mills, John Walsh, and two men Bud didn't know were lounging in uncomfortable-looking straight-backed wooden chairs pulled up around a battered oak table.

Joe Ring began the meeting with an announcement. "Constable Milling has put his house in Rosmalley up for sale." Bud heard a few indrawn breaths but no one said anything, and Joe went on.

"That's not as positive as it sounds. We assumed that burnin' his yacht would be clear warnin' that he should leave

Ireland, but we just learned that he's bought a home in Westport, on Newport Road, so he could be better protected." Joe paused and surveyed the room. "But if that's what the constable is thinkin', we're goin' to show him otherwise."

The assembled men murmured among themselves. "What are we goin' to do about it, Joe?" Rick Mills asked, nervously shifting his bulk on the hard, wooden chair.

"This time we're goin' to do more than scare him," Joe said slowly. "This time we're goin' to assassinate Constable John Milling."

Bud sucked in his breath. *This is daft. We'll all end up dead or in prison.* He glanced at the men around the table. Only a few showed any apprehension; most looked resolved.

"Kevin," Ring said, "I'm goin' to need some help from your family."

Kevin straightened. "You name it. What do you need?"

"I've been watchin' Constable Milling. He winds his clocks about ten, just before he turns in. His kids are already sleepin', and his wife is gettin' ready for bed. He'll be alone in their front sittin' room. So, tomorrow night around ten, we're goin' to pay a visit to Constable Milling."

"What do you plan to do?" Terry Ludden asked.

"Kill him."

Dead silence.

"Kill him, how?" Terry pursued.

Ring drew in a long breath. "We can see into the sittin' room from the woods across the road from his house. We wait 'til we're sure he's alone, and then we shoot him from there."

Bud closed his hands into fists. Murder? Jesus, I've had enough of killing. He felt pulled in two directions. Part of him wanted nothing to do with killing a man in cold blood. But another part of him wanted an Ireland where he wasn't called a 'mick', where he could get a job and build a good life with Rose.

"We?" someone asked. "Who's 'we'?"

Joe didn't answer, and the question just hung there. Instead, Ring changed the subject. "The IRA thinks it's time we make British officials the target of our fight. We're an Irish army dedicated to fightin' for our country, and that country has established its capital in Dublin with our own parliament. Now's the time to drive our enemy out of Ireland." He paused and looked around. "Are you all with me?"

Joe's challenge met with shouts and cheers. Despite his trepidation, Bud had to admit he felt a glimmer of hope. He hadn't felt such a clear sense of the power of rightness since he'd fought in France. Then another, stronger emotion, welled up in him—his love for Rose. This would be for Rose, for all the years of their life together in an Ireland that was free.

Joe punched his fist in the air. "Our movement will strike not only in Westport but in other places in Ireland. We're doin' our part for our country."

"We're with you, Joe," red-haired Rick Mills shouted.

Joe smiled. "Whenever any of us are seen in Westport, there's a good chance we'll be stopped and searched. We'll be on the street next to Newport Road, and I need one of you Ryans to bring us three handguns. Bring them to me there."

Now Bud, too, wondered who Joe mean by "we."

"Will you need us to stick around and take the guns back?" Kevin asked.

"That will not be necessary. After you give us the guns, get out of the area. We'll make our escape the best way we can." Joe stood and looked around the room. "Are there any other questions?"

Another long silence. Bud noted that Joe Ring answered only the questions he wanted to, so no one was to know who the assassins were. Smart man.

"Fine," Joe said with a grin. "Let's put this plan into action."

* * *

On the night of the planned assassination, customer flow at the tavern was light. Bud worked behind the bar with Mike, noticing that every time the tavern door opened, a gust of wind laced with swirling snow blew in.

"It's bloody cold out there," one customer complained. "That wind blows right through ya. Pour me a shot of brandy now, will you? I'm needin' to get me toes warm."

Bud pushed a glass at him and poured him a shot. Other customers complained about the weather, and they all wanted the same, often chased by a pint of beer.

About half past nine, Rose walked in, bundled up against the snowstorm in a heavy coat and a wool muffler. Bud kissed her, then slid her coat off. "What are you doin' here on a night like this?" he asked.

Without a word, she marched to the back of the tavern carrying her coat and muffler, and motioned for him to follow. "What's goin' on?" he hissed.

"My brothers told me about the plan tonight. I'm goin' with you to deliver the guns."

A heavy feeling of dread settled in his chest. He didn't want Rose involved in any shooting. "Are you daft?" he snapped. "If anyone sees us out in this weather on the same night Constable Milling is killed, they'll know we were part of it."

She just looked at him. "You're not goin' alone."

"I *am* going alone. You're not part of this plan, Rose. It's dangerous, and I don't want you gettin' caught up in it. I can't have anything happen to you."

She pressed her lips together in a way Bud was beginning to recognize. His Rose was stubborn. Not just stubborn, he amended; she was foolhardy. While he admired her courage, this whole operation was risky. And, oh God, what if she got hurt?

"Ring's not goin' to try anythin' in this weather," she said. "He'll probably call the whole thing off."

"Maybe. But I said I'd bring guns, and my word is to be trusted. But I want you to stay here and wait for me. And ..." he added sternly, "that's not a matter that up for discussion."

He left her sitting at the back table, climbed the stairs to his bedroom, and pulled on a pair of heavy wool trousers and a thick sweater. Then he added a bulky overcoat and loaded three .38 revolvers into his pockets. When he came back downstairs, Rose was still sitting at the back table. She had not put on her coat or muffler, which made Bud feel better. He kissed her and without a word headed out the back door.

He hadn't walked more than five blocks when he heard a familiar voice. "Hey, Ryan. Over here."

He spun around to see three dark shadows huddled together near Grady's market. "Joe?"

"Yeah," a low voice said. "Did you bring the revolvers?"

Bud hesitated. *Am I really doing this? Risking my life to kill some constable?* Before he let himself think about it, he handed over the guns.

"Thanks, Bud. Wish us luck."

He shook their hands in silence, then he turned back toward the tavern. When he walked in, the first thing he did was look for Rose. She wasn't at the back table, and a cold feeling flooded into his belly. "Kevin, where's Rose?"

His brother slid a pint down the bar to a customer. "She took off after you."

"What?"

"She followed you out the back door. Didn't you see her?"

"No, I didn't see her." Without another word, he went back out into the storm and headed for Grady's market where he'd met Joe Ring. Just as he reached it, several shots rang out. His breathing stopped. *Rose! She's out there somewhere.*

Frantically he looked everywhere, but there was no sign of her. With a sinking feeling he decided to go back to the tavern, and wait for her there. When he walked in, he spoke to no one, went upstairs, and shed his coat and scarf. Then he came down and took his place behind the bar with Kevin.

His heart pounding, he waited agonizing minutes for

Rose to walk in the door. *Where was she?*

A new customer came in, a regular Bud recognized, and ordered a beer. "Did you hear the shots?"

Bud went cold all over. "Shots?" Kevin said blandly, shaking his head. "Shots where?"

"Over near the Newport Road." The man swallowed a mouthful of brew and shook his head. "Now, I ask you, who would be out in this storm shootin' off a gun?"

"Did you see anyone out there?" Bud asked.

The man sent him a puzzled look. "You kiddin'? Would you draw me another beer?"

For the rest of the night Bud poured shots of whiskey and sent foaming glasses of beer sliding down the bar to the patrons, but all the while he kept his eyes on the back door, praying Rose would walk through it any minute. *When I see her, so help me I'm going to … What? Rose doesn't dance to your tune, boyo. Not yet, anyway.*

Oh, Jesus, where in the hell is she?

Chapter Eight

An Arrest

When the clock struck midnight, Rose was still missing. Bud tried to stay calm, but finally he couldn't stand it any longer. He had to go out and look for her again. Just at that moment Deputy Constable Harris and another constable stepped into the tavern, bringing a blast of cold air and a swirl of snow.

"Hey," Kevin shouted, "close that door!"

Harris backtracked and pulled the door shut.

"What can we do for you, Constables?" Kevin folded a bar towel and laid it near the sink.

Constable Harris blew out his breath and rubbed his hands together. "Has anyone come into the tavern in the last hour?"

Kevin looked at Bud, and they both shrugged. "I don't know," Kevin said. "We were too busy to pay much attention."

I'm sure not going to inform on any of our own customers. "Would you be lookin' for someone in particular?" Bud asked.

The constable didn't answer. Instead, both men tramped up and down the length of the suddenly quiet bar, scanning the patrons. "Who are you lookin' for, Constable?" Kevin repeated with irritation. "What's goin' on?"

Both officers took their time walking back to the entrance. "There's been a shooting—"

Before he could finish, another constable burst in.

"We're wanted back at the station," he panted. "We think we've got the shooter."

Oh my God, have they arrested Rose?

Another blast of cold air swept the room, and the door banged shut behind them. Bud stuck his head out the front door and peered up and down the deserted street until Kevin shouted at him. "Bud, get back in here and close that door!"

"Did you hear what that deputy said, Kev? He said they caught the shooter."

"I heard. He said 'shooter,' singular. Either they made a mistake or they only got one of them."

"Yeah, you're right. Guess that's a good sign, is it?" he said in a tight voice. "Kev, can you handle things here? I'm going back out and look for Rose again."

He raced upstairs, donned his coat and wound his wool muffler around his neck, then retrieved his Eveready electric torch from the cellar and slipped out the back door. Oh, God, *I hope she didn't try to walk home. For sure she'd get lost in this storm.*

He took a circuitous route through the woods near Constable Millings' house, scanning the area with the flashlight. Suddenly someone tapped him on the shoulder. Startled, he dropped the torch in the snow. When he swung around, Deputy Harris stood before him.

"Jaysus, you scared me!"

"Sorry, Bud." The deputy picked up the flashlight, wiped off the slush, and handed it back. "What are you doing out in this storm so late?"

"Just restless, I guess. Stretchin' my legs. Not much business in the tavern tonight. Heard you made an arrest in that shootin'."

"That I can't tell you. Somebody shot up Constable Milling's house, like I said, but names are confidential until we know who actually pulled the trigger. It's bad business, shooting up people's houses. We've got someone at the station for questioning now, so we'll soon get to the bottom of it. You see or hear anything suspicious?"

"Haven't heard a thing, Constable." He was tempted to ask Harris if he had seen Rose, then thought better of it. He sure wasn't going to tell him that Rose had been out tonight. For all he knew, she was with Joe Ring.

"Sure is nasty out tonight," Harris said, rubbing his upper arms. "You should get inside, Bud."

"You're right."

He walked straight back to the bar. The last customer had left, but to his relief there was Rose, huddled at the back table, her teeth chattering and her hands cradling a mug of hot tea. He ran to her, lifted her out of her chair, and folded his arms around her. Her whole body was shivering, and he rubbed her back to warm her up.

"Rose! Where in God's name have you been? I've been lookin' all over for you. I was so worried I thought I was goin' to have a heart attack."

"I was h-hidin'."

"What? Hidin' from who?"

"I was across from Constable Millings' house l-looking for you when I heard the sh-shooting start. I headed back here, but the constables were runnin' out of the station, and I had to hide. I couldn't move around in the s-snow or I would have been seen, and they'd want to know what I was doing out there, so I just s-sat down right where I was and tried not to move. I hid my gun in the woods in case someone found me." She sat back down and wrapped both hands around the mug of tea, but Bud noticed she didn't drink any.

"I'm still c-cold, Bud. Could you get my coat?"

He draped it around her shoulders, and she tugged it tight across her body. "I saw them arrest Chuck Gavin."

Chuck Gavin? Was he even at the meeting where Joe Ring set this up?

"Anybody else?"

"I don't think so." Kevin appeared from the kitchen with a hot bowl of mutton stew. "Oh, Kevin, thank you!" She spooned up the stew in silence while Kevin closed up the tavern and went upstairs.

Bud convinced her it was safer to stay in their secret cellar room than try to get home in the storm. After a long pause she nodded, laid her spoon in the empty bowl, and followed him down the cellar stairs to the secret room. She shed her coat and curled up under a blanket on one of the cots.

Bud stretched out beside her and wrapped her in his arms. He kissed her, but she was too cold and tired to even kiss him back. He lay awake beside her, thanking God she was not hurt, then began to wonder about Constable Milling. *Was he dead? Injured? Maybe even unhurt?*

In the morning before anyone was awake, Bud walked

down to the market and picked up the morning edition of the Mayo News. "Constable John Milling Shot," the headline read. He quickly scanned the article to learn that Milling was still alive but seriously wounded.

He raced back to the tavern where he found Kevin, Mike, and Rose gathered at the back table eating bacon rashers, fried eggs, and white pudding.

"I got the newspaper." He tossed it down on the table and grabbed a fork. "John Milling survived the shootin'." He slid some bacon and a fried egg onto his plate.

"We know," Kevin said. "Joe Ring came by early this mornin'. There's a meetin' at his farm in an hour. Bring that paper, Bud. And I think Rose should come with us and tell Joe what she saw last night."

They took a horse carriage to the snow-covered Ring farmhouse, which was surrounded by other carriages, saddled horses, and Joe Gill's Renault. When they walked in, both Alan and Terry Ludden leaped to their feet and threw their arms around Rose. "We were that worried when you didn't come home, Rose," Alan blurted. "Maggie's beside herself."

"I wasn't thinkin'," she said. "I was tired and cold and ... well, I just wanted to get some sleep, so I stayed at the tavern."

Her brothers raised their eyebrows, but neither one said

a word.

Bud slapped the Mayo News down on the table. "You've seen this?"

"We've seen it," Joe Ring said tersely. "Last night we tried to kill John Milling, but we failed. But we're coordinatin' our efforts all over Ireland, and Dublin reports that last night Alan Bell--he's a magistrate and a member of the British Secret Service and he's been a real thorn in our side. Anyway, last night Bell was grabbed off a Dublin tram and shot. I'm thinkin' his death makes us more secure."

Those assembled around the table murmured quietly. Bud flinched but kept silent.

"How come you didn't kill Milling?" Rick Mills asked, shoving his red hair out of his eyes.

Apparently, Ring didn't like the question. He looked sideways at Mills. "I don't think we should have used .38's. From now on, we use .45's. Now the question is whether we should make another attempt on Constable Milling."

Joe Walsh shook his head. "We need to give this a few days rest. We put a lot of lead into Milling—he may still die from his wounds. Be a miracle if he survives."

At that moment the sound of a galloping horse made everyone freeze, and after a tense minute, farmer John O'Hern rushed in. "John Milling's dead!" he announced breathlessly. "He died this morning."

Joe Ring smiled. "Good. It's too bad it came to this, but the English don't understand anythin' but violence, so it's violence we'll give them. Now we need to decide what to do next. We need targets. Keep in mind that our efforts are against the British authorities. I've a few ideas, but I want all of you to think about where we should strike next."

The men discussed some possibilities, but after the news about Milling, no one felt much like making any definite plans, and the meeting ended in strained silence.

The next morning, Bud picked up a copy of the Mayo News, took it back to the tavern, and called Kevin and Mike over. "Look at this."

"Martial law has been declared in Ireland," Bud read aloud. "Minister of Defense, Winston Churchill, announced today that he has named a group of ex-military men to be deployed as deputy constables in every county in Ireland. The action was taken in response to the murders of Constable John Milling in Westport and magistrate Alan Bell in Dublin."

"Christ almighty!" Kevin swore. "The fat's in the fire now for sure."

* * *

On Wednesday the first of the new deputies arrived in

Westport. Bud watched with Rose and other Westport residents as three troop trucks from Dublin dropped off 20 or so uniformed men, accompanied by something new, an armored car. Outside the police station, three Westport deputy constables surveyed the scene.

The tunics of the new men were dark green, so dark that from even a short distance away they looked black. The matching hats had a small leather strap around the base and a visor covered in the same dark green material. They wore leather belts around their waists, leather cartridge belts across their chests, and British khaki riding pants with wrapped leggings like the ones Bud had worn in France. All were armed with new revolvers carried in leather holsters.

"Hey, Constable Harris," Bud called out. "What's this all about? I've never seen black and tan uniforms before."

Harris wandered over to where Bud and Rose stood. "Those men are the Royal Irish Constabulary Special Reserve, all combat veterans from France and Flanders. We had half a dozen turn up yesterday." He lowered his voice and bent toward Bud. "They're a rough bunch. Boasting and bragging about how they're going to clean up Westport, put a final end to our problems. I don't have a good feeling about this."

He straightened up just as one of the soldiers, a sergeant, purposely bumped into Rose. When she yelped, the soldier growled, "Get outta my way, mick."

Bud squared off against the man, but he was quickly surrounded by three of the sergeant's mates, and one shoved Bud from behind. He spun around, fist cocked, but Constable Harris stepped between them. "That's enough!" he shouted.

"He pushed my girl," Bud protested.

Harris pulled out his baton and separated the men. "Move along, now."

The soldiers joined others gathered at the rear of the first truck and began unloading a long, cylindrical device. It took four of them to lug it into the police station.

"What is that?" Rose asked. "I've never seen anything like that."

"That's a Jennings machine gun," Bud explained. "I saw a lot of them in France."

She wrapped her hand around his forearm. "A machine gun? What do they need a machine gun for?"

Bud shook his head. "I don't know." But he did know. *Those men are here to wage war. I don't think Joe Ring has a clue about what he's up against.*

A second Jennings machine gun was unloaded, followed by crates of ammunition, boxes of rifles, and more cartridges. Then the empty trucks turned around and headed out of town.

"They've had no police training," Constable Harris mused. "All they've had is the training they got in the military."

Bud said nothing, just looked at Harris.

"They call themselves 'reinforcements'," the constable added. "But maybe you remember that old saying, 'Be afraid when someone shows up and says 'We're from the government and we're here to help'."

As they watched, the armored car was parked behind the police station next to the black squad car, and the black and tan uniformed soldiers filed into police headquarters.

* * *

That Friday night Bud trudged home in the snow, exhausted from a day of searching for work and sick of being refused because he was a 'mick'. Even though he was late for his shift behind the bar, he paused to watch the lamplighter moving silently down the line of poles in the business district. As the man's hook opened each gas valve, he deftly swiveled the wick so the flame would ignite the hissing gas. The simple, familiar operation had a calming effect. *Even when everything is falling apart all around us, the street lamps still need to be lit.*

The tavern was crowded, and he rushed upstairs to shed

his coat and to tie on an apron. When he arrived back at the bar, a group of six Black and Tans were seated in the back, and they were getting loud. Kevin, balancing a steel serving tray, was collecting the empty glasses when one of the soldiers grabbed his arm. "Bring us six more," he snarled

"I think it's time you fellas slowed down a bit," Kevin responded.

The soldier shot to his feet. "Goddamned mick bartenders," he slurred. "Who d'ya think yer talking to?" He shoved Kevin, who stumbled backward trying to balance his tray. Two of the empties tumbled to the floor and broke.

All conversation ceased. Mike rushed over to sweep up the glass, keeping an eye on the table of drunks. Bud moved behind the bar, closer to the shotgun they kept under the counter.

"What are we goin' to do?" Kevin muttered when Mike had cleaned up the mess.

Bud moved to the end of the bar nearest the front door and grabbed the forearm of a customer he knew. "Liam," he murmured, "go get the deputy constable."

Liam slid off his stool and disappeared into the street.

Chapter Nine

Retribution

Bud watched the Tans guzzling their beer, then suggested to Kevin that they should send them on their way. "They're gettin' pretty rowdy, and we don't want any trouble. I sent Liam to get the deputy constable."

"You're right," Kevin agreed. "It's time to close their party down." He walked over to the table of soldiers and held up his hand. "Gentlemen, you've had a good time tonight. Now I think maybe it's time to wind it down and go on home."

"Do ya, now, mick?" one soldier shot back. "Well maybe we're not finished drinking."

"I say you are finished," Kevin said, his voice quiet.

At that, the soldier flung his half-empty beer glass at him. Kevin ducked, and the glass shattered against the wall behind him. An uneasy silence settled over the tavern crowd, and Bud felt under the bar for the shotgun and braced himself for trouble.

Kevin faced the soldier. "All right, that's enough. It's time to go."

One of the Tans jumped up, grabbed a wooden chair, and smashed it on the table until it broke into pieces. "Took ya two tries," taunted one of his mates. The other soldiers laughed.

Bud stepped out from behind the bar and leveled the pump-action shotgun at the table. "Stand down," he shouted. He dodged another beer glass hurled in his direction, and then he pulled the trigger. The blast was deafening. Buckshot sprayed over the soldiers' heads and put a hole in the back wall. The other customers hit the floor, and every single Tan at the table raised his hands in the air.

When Bud pumped the shotgun and ejected the empty shell casing, one of the Tans reached for his holstered revolver. Bud swung his weapon toward him and shook his head. "No, you don't, mate."

At that moment, Head Constable Keith Gray and a pair of armed deputy constables burst in the front door. "What's going on in here?" he demanded. He pointed at Bud. "Put that thing away, Ryan."

Bud lowered the shotgun but kept a tight grip on it.

"Sergeant Clark," Constable Gray shouted. "Explain yourself."

One of the soldiers jerked to his feet and saluted. "Jus' hav'n a bit of fun, now," he said sheepishly.

The constable nodded. "Get your men back to the barracks," he ordered. "*Now*."

"Yessir," the sergeant mumbled.

Kevin stepped forward. "Don't come back to this tavern," he warned.

One of the privates spun to face him. "We'll damn well go where we wanna go, mick."

Constable Gray waved him out. "Let's go," he repeated. All six soldiers headed for the entrance, glaring at Kevin and Bud as they passed.

"What about the damage they caused?" Kevin asked.

The constable faced him. "I apologize for their behavior. Send me a bill for the damage."

"Includin' that hole in the wall?"

"Who put it there?" Constable Gray asked. "One of the Tans?"

"I did," Bud volunteered. "I fired a shotgun to get their attention."

Gray jerked his thumb at him. "Then you can pay for it."

He and the two deputies turned on their heels and marched out after the soldiers.

When the customers began to resume their seats, Kevin raised his hand. "Sorry about all the excitement, mates. The next round is on us."

Bud set the shotgun on the bar and reloaded before he slipped it back in its hiding place. "Kevin, I'll clean up the rest of the mess before we close, but can you take the bar? Walter Ring and the Ludden sisters are comin' over."

"No problem, Bud."

A few minutes later Walter strolled in with Maggie and Rose. "What happened in here?" Walter asked, studying the broken chair and shards of glass.

Bud paused while sweeping up the broken glass. "Oh, some of the Tans were here. They had a bit too much to drink and got a little rowdy." While he finished cleaning up the spilled beer and the smashed chair, Walter and the two girls took an empty table in the back.

"Walter," Bud said when he joined them. "Does Joe Ring know about those machine guns the Tans unloaded yesterday?"

Walter nodded. "He knows," he said shortly. "Not much goes on in Westport that Joe Ring doesn't know about."

Rose tugged on Bud's arm. "There's a dance at the church tonight, Bud. Let's go and forget about all this, just for a few hours."

Bud said nothing. He'd just fired a shotgun in his family's tavern, and that didn't make him feel like dancing, even with Rose. But she stood up, took him by the hand, and led him outside.

"Let's go have a little fun, Bud."

"You know I'm goin' to have to fix that hole tomorrow mornin'."

Rose frowned. "I'm thinkin' you need to get your mind off the bar. She stepped in close and rose on her tiptoes to kiss his cheek. "Please, Bud."

He had a hard time whenever Rose kissed him and said "please." He took her in his arms, but even holding her close couldn't get some things off his mind. He didn't feel good about the way things were developing. *That machine gun the Tans unloaded means big trouble for sure.*

After a long moment, he nodded, and Rose snuggled close. "Bud, darlin'," she whispered, "you need to relax."

"Yeah, I guess you're right."

Half an hour later Maggie and Walter, together with Rose and Bud, walked into St. Mary's church hall, alive with music and conversation. He pulled Rose into a slow two-step and tried to get his mind off the Tans.

"You know somethin'?" he whispered after a few minutes. "My gut's tellin' me this won't be the end. None of

Joe Ring's people are in the mood to let this drop."

"Well, I'm in the mood to forget all about it for the next two hours."

"I'll try," he whispered. "But I know this won't be the end. No one is in the mood to let this drop."

"Bud, stop thinking about it."

"Yeah." He kissed her neck and kept dancing.

* * *

The next morning, he rose early and went downstairs to fix the hole he'd put in the wall. Suddenly, he heard a commotion outside, and when he peered through the window he saw six Tans loading one of the Jennings machine guns into the constable's squad car. Then all six soldiers piled into the vehicle and sped off.

Now I wonder what that's all about. Looks for all the world like they're starting a bloody war.

He tried to put it out of his mind, finished putting a temporary patch over the hole in the wall, and then walked down to the hardware store for plaster and a pint of paint to finish the job. Just as he emerged back onto the street, the black squad car careened up the street, and the six Tans tumbled out.

"Well done!" one shouted to his mates. They shook

hands all around and slapped each other on the back. "That'll show those micks not to mess with us," one of them chortled.

They then unloaded the Jennings.

Jesus, what have they done?

He needed to get word of this to Joe Ring, so he went back to the tavern and found Kevin. A minute later, Kevin was out the back door, and Bud wiped down the bar to open for business.

The morning hours passed without event, but by late afternoon when Kevin hadn't returned, Bud knew something was up. It was still light out when he heard someone knocking at the back door. He unlocked it to find an ashen-faced Joe Ring and his brothers, Walter and Jack. Without a word, they stepped inside. Old Mike Greene and his wrinkle-faced wife Mary Ellen were right behind them, and before he could close the door, a somber Ludden family entourage—Alan, Terry, Maggie, and Rose, streamed in. Bud's belly tightened.

Rose hugged him, but she didn't say anything. Her face looked white and tense.

"What's happened?" he asked.

"You haven't heard?" Rose whispered. "The Tans paid a visit to the Mills farm. And they ..." She stopped and swallowed hard. "They machine-gunned Rick and his wife,

Trish, and ..." Her voice broke. "And they killed their four-year-old daughter, Ashlyn."

"What?" Bud felt the blood drain from his head. "Why?"

"The Greenes live a half mile from the Mills farm," she went on, her voice unsteady. "When they heard machine gun fire comin' from the farm and saw smoke, Mike saddled his horse and rode to the Rings to get help." She drew in a shaky breath. "When Mike and Joe Ring reached the farm, they found Rick's body. The farmhouse was on fire, and when they got the fire under control, they found Trish and Ashlyn's bodies inside."

Bud clenched his fists and turned away. *So that's what those damned Tans were crowing about. That's just murder, pure and simple.*

Rose put her hand on his back. "I know how you feel, Bud."

He spun toward her. "No, you don't. Why would they do somethin' like that?"

"We don't know," Joe Ring said.

By this time, more IRA members had arrived, along with some of their wives. All the seats at the bar and those at the back tables were filled, so people stood along the walls.

Joe Ring finally stood up. "Does anyone know what this shootin' was all about?"

Tim McGowan pushed his tall frame away from the wall.

"After we shot John Milling, Constable Gray gave the Black and Tans a list of IRA suspects. Like most of us here in this room, Rick Mills was on that list." His ordinarily quiet voice grew harsh. "Could be the Tans went out to the Mills farm to arrest him."

"But why bring a machine gun?" Joe asked, raising his voice.

"And why kill Trish and Ashlyn?" Rose pursued.

Brigit Gill nervously smoothed one hand over her long, copper-colored braids. "Do you think they plan to kill us all?"

"I don't think so," McGowan responded. He shifted his lanky body from foot to foot. "I think the visit to the Mills place was in retaliation for Constable Milling's death. It was meant as a warnin' to all of us."

"Maybe if they think they're even now everything will calm down," Rose said softly.

"Like hell," Ring declared, slamming his fist on the table. "But first things first. Let's get the Mills family buried, and after the funeral we'll talk about this again."

Joe Walsh leaned his bulk against the bar. "I say we hit them now."

"No!" Joe Ring snapped. "I say when we hit them, and I say how. Right now, we all need to calm down, and then later we will make a plan and act. Does everyone understand?"

* * *

When word spread about the killings of the Mills family, Catholics from all over northwestern Ireland came to Westport for the wake and the funeral. No sooner was the service over than rumors started flying about another Westport IRA Column forming to fight the Black and Tans. The day after the burial, a small group of people met at the Ring farm. But this time, Bud saw something he hadn't seen before--armed guards on top of the knoll shielding the Ring farmhouse. And Joe Ring had posted a guard patrolling in front of the house, armed with a shotgun.

The meeting included the Ring brothers, all four Ludden siblings, Tim McGowan and his equally lanky brother Kevin, Joe and Brigit Gill, and Mike McGwire and his very pregnant wife, Sheila. When Bud sat down at a table next to Rose, she remarked on the guards posted around the house.

"I noticed."

"We can't afford guards around our farm," she confided. "So, we're all takin' turns watchin' the house all night. But we know we can't keep that up, so we've found hidin' places in case the Tans come."

Bud reached over and squeezed her hand. "Don't forget the cellar room at the tavern," he whispered.

Ring began the meeting on a cautionary note. "A lot of people want to hit back at the Tans," he said. "But I'm sayin' we bide our time. Another rebel group has formed in Westport, callin' themselves the East Westport Flying Column. That makes us the West Flying Column."

"Who's in that East group?" asked McGwire, scratching his dark beard.

Joe leveled a long look at him. "You know better than to ask a question like that, Mike. There's no reason for us to know who's in that group. Besides, I want to hit the Tans with *our* group. Rick Mills and his family were *our* people."

A long silence fell, and then Joe changed the subject. "Ladies, we're goin' to need your help."

Every woman in the room sat up straighter.

Ring leveled his gaze at them. "I want to set up an ambush on the Mills farm road. There's a stretch of highway about half a mile this side of their farm that passes between two low hills. That's a good spot for an ambush. It's the only road that leads to and from the farm, so no innocent bystanders will get in the way."

"And you want my sister Maggie and me to make sure of this?" Rose asked.

Joe shook his head. "I want you women to spread a rumor that the Westport Flying Column is goin' to meet at the burned-out Mills farmhouse this Friday to plan a retaliation strike. Tell everyone this meetin's goin' to be midmorning Friday, and that it's secret. That should lure the Tans out to the farm."

"How will you know exactly when they're comin'?" someone asked.

"We'll set up the ambush and then we'll just wait all mornin'."

Bud spoke up. "I think you should post a lookout on the road leadin' into that little valley. If the Tans send more than one car, or if they send an armored car, you should let them through unmolested and plan another ambush. You don't have the firepower to take on an armored car. But if they send that squad car, the lookout should give a signal."

Joe nodded. "Anything else?"

Bud hesitated. *I thought when I was done with France, I was done with killing.* But here I go again. "You should station four riflemen behind one hill, and as the car passes, fire into it. Two men need to aim for the driver, and the rest of the rifles should aim for the front passenger and those in the rear seat."

Joe Gill smoothed his pale mustache and frowned. "What about the machine gun? What if they bring that?"

"It takes a while to set that thing up," Bud responded. "The riflemen should kill everyone in the car before they can bring the machine gun into action."

"And," Joe Ring added, "then we capture that machine gun and any cartridges they're carryin'."

"What about the livestock on the Mills farm?" Maggie asked.

"Good question. Mike McGwire should go over there and bring any animals to his place. We need to keep the livestock out of the hands of the English."

Joe then divided the men into two rifle squads, careful to include experienced marksmen in each group. Then he selected Tim and Kevin McGowan to serve as lookouts. "We'll meet at the Mills farm Friday before dawn and get set up. And there will be a few more friends who will join us."

He then turned toward Bud. "Bud, I want you and your brother Kevin to bring fourteen rifles and some .45's from the guns stored in your cellar. Be sure to bring enough ammunition. Bud, take a ride out to the Mills farm road and scout the ambush site. See if there's anythin' I missed."

Without thinking, Bud saluted.

Another long silence fell, and he found himself studying the faces of those assembled. None of them, except maybe Joe Ring, knew a tinker's damn about what this could lead to.

Chapter Ten

Ambush

Bud left the meeting with the same sense of foreboding he'd felt during every pre-battle meeting in France—dread of what might happen and his determination to get the job done. He took a deep breath and stuffed down the anxiety that welled up whenever a military operation was about to begin.

But, he reflected, this was different from fighting in the trenches in France because now he was at home and Rose was with him. The fight for Ireland was a fight for her. For them, this fight was personal, and Rose made the struggle worth whatever it took.

The next morning, he borrowed a horse from Keough

Stables and rode out to the Mills farm road. The countryside was shrouded in fog, and the cold, damp air penetrated his entire body, making his injured hip throb and his lungs hurt when he breathed. His route was along a rutted dirt road, now a muddy quagmire from the melting snow. He reined the horse in at the top of the adjoining hill and dismounted.

The stretch of road leading into the small valley and the Mills farm was straight, with no curves. The lookout would be able to see the police car coming from a long distance away, and there was enough scrub vegetation that Tim and Kevin McGowan would have plenty of cover.

He remounted and rode down from the top of the hill, noting that the elevation was high enough so men firing their rifles would be aiming downward, not across to the other side. This hill could shield the men from view, but the opposite hills were flatter, so that in order to be hidden, the riflemen would have to stay hidden back about 20 feet. When the time came, they would advance from their hiding place, drop into firing position, and unleash their volley.

Leading his horse, he limped across the road to check out any other hidden dangers. He saw none. The morning fog was beginning to lift, and he pulled his peacoat tighter. He liked the peace and solitude of the Irish countryside, with cattle and sheep grazing in the distance, and he loved the quiet. The land was beautiful, even in winter.

He remounted and rode back down to the road and turned toward Ludden Farm, working out ambush contingencies on the way. When he reached the Ludden's, Alan stepped out of the barn carrying a rifle on his shoulder. "Hey, Bud. Top of the mornin' to ya. What are you doin' out here so early?"

Bud dismounted and shook his hand. "I was scoutin' the Mills farm road for the ambush."

"Rose will want to see you, so come on in for some tea."

Inside, Joe Ludden tossed a peat brick on the fire just as Rose walked in. "Bud! What are you doin' here?" She wound her arms around his neck and gave him a kiss.

"I just rode out to Mills farm to check things out." He drew in a long breath. "Joe Ring picked a good spot for the ambush. The Tans should fall right into the trap."

Rose furrowed her brow. "You seem ... different. What's wrong?"

"My hip wound is botherin' me some this mornin'. Makes me limp."

She looked straight into his eyes. "There's something else, isn't there?"

He took her elbow. "Could we go somewhere private?"

Rose steered him to a quiet corner of the house and sat him down, then pulled up a chair opposite him. "What's botherin' you?" she whispered.

He looked away. "It's the ambush. I know we can't let the British Tans murder Catholic families to protect the Protestant ascendency. But their terror tactics are havin' the opposite effect; Catholics all over Ireland are fighting back. Joe Ring has a good plan, but the men we'll be facin' are ex-soldiers. I might have served in the trenches with some of 'em, and now I'm plannin' to kill them? It doesn't feel right, Rose."

She took his hand but said nothing.

"When I was wounded, all I wanted to do was forget the war, come home, get a job, and marry you. Now I find myself still killin' people. And I've got no job, and we're no closer to getting' married."

For a long moment she said nothing, then she lifted her head and held his gaze. "I don't want you to be a part of this ambush, Bud."

"Not much I can do about that now," he said quietly.

"But there is! Let's get away, go to America. Lots of the Irish are emigratin', and it would just be like bein' here in Ireland, but without the hatred and the violence."

He took both her hands in his and shook his head. "I can't, Rose. I just can't. For the first time in centuries, Ireland has a real chance to be independent from England, but Winston Churchill won't have it. He's recruited unemployed ex-military men from England, Scotland, and

Wales to terrorize us and keep us from havin' our republic. We have a parliament, and we have Irishmen all over the country fightin' for independence. If we can drive the Tans out, the British government will go with them. But I'm afraid they'll not go without more bloodshed."

"But—"

"Rose, Ireland can be free! And we can make it happen." He squeezed her hands. "I hope you understand, Rose. I have to do this."

* * *

Very late the following night, Bud finished his shift at the tavern, closed up, and headed out in pre-dawn darkness to the Mills farm road, along with Mike and Kevin, in Joe Gill's Renault. They found the rest of their mates waiting for them, signaling with their flashlights. Joe parked the car out of sight.

Kevin, Mike, and Bud distributed the rifles and .45's Bud had collected, and he slipped his own .45 under his belt. The McGowan brothers each took a .45 and started down the road to the lookout point. The men assigned to the opposite side of the road were already in place.

They waited as the sun rose on a misty morning. Hours passed. The sun burned off the fog to reveal a clear blue sky, and the men on Bud's side of the road made quiet, nervous conversation. Just as he eased himself down onto the grass to take the weight off his hip, Joe Walsh spoke.

"There's the signal."

Joe Ring waved to the men on the other side of the road to get down, and Bud watched a black dot move toward them. The vehicle was too quiet to be the massive armored car with a machine gun, and Bud thanked God it was the squad car. He looked across to the opposite hill and saw that all the men were well hidden. His own men lay in prone position behind the ridge, waiting for the black dot to come into focus.

"Don't fire until I tell you to," Joe Ring whispered.

Bud aimed his rifle and waited. The black dot grew larger, and he could see that the police car was alone. *This is it.*

The sound of the automobile engine grew louder, and Bud tightened his grip on his revolver. He allowed for wind and distance, held his breath, and waited for Joe's command. Adrenaline pumped through his body.

He stole a look at the other men. Every one of them was staring at Joe Ring, and Ring was focused on the advancing automobile. *If they don't take steady aim and maintain it, they're going to miss.*

"Fire!"

Bud sighted, squeezed the trigger, and six other rifles exploded. He put two more rounds into the windshield of the car, then ducked down and took cover. A short volley burst from the opposite hill, and then Joe Ring was up and running toward the car.

What the hell is he doing?

The squad car lurched off the road and came to a stop. Bud got to his feet and started down the slope, slowed by his aching hip. The rest of the men and the entire group from the opposite hill were converging on the car. When Joe reached it, he began firing into the interior. When the men's rifles were empty, they used their .45's and kept firing.

By the time Bud reached the squad car, the bodies inside were so shot up they were unrecognizable. He closed his eyes. In the military he'd learned to conserve ammunition, but in a frenzy of bloodlust these amateurs had emptied their weapons into the Tans, who were already dead. Two of the four men in the Ford wore deputy constable uniforms. The inside of the car was a mess, but it didn't contain the Jennings machine gun.

Young Tim Keough stepped away, bent over, and vomited. Bud's brother, Kevin, watched him, then shoved Bud to one side and threw up on the grass. Joe Ring ignored them.

"Take their identification papers and their weapons," he

yelled. "Then let's get this mess cleaned up and get out of here."

Bud looked around at the men's ashen faces and watched Kevin wipe his mouth with his sleeve. "You all right?" he murmured.

"Yeah. Fine."

He's not fine. None of us are fine. Now they know what killing is all about.

He collected an armload of rifles, limped over the hill, and stashed them in Joe Gill's Renault. Gill was right behind him with another load, and then Ring appeared with a fistful of blood-soaked identification papers. Bud noticed he wasn't smiling.

"Mike Greene," Ring ordered, "I want you to go into town and report that gunshots were heard comin' from the Mills farm. Tell everyone that you didn't dare go over there because of the shootin' last week. Got it?"

"Got it." Greene mounted his horse and trotted away to the north. The rest of the men dispersed in all directions. Bud slipped into the Renault next to Kevin, who was shaking. "I didn't expect that," his brother said as they headed back to Westport. "I've never seen bodies mangled like that."

Joe Gill dropped them off at the tavern's back door and promised to come back after dark and unload the weapons.

The minute the three Ryan brothers entered, they headed for the bar. Bud picked up a beer glass and sent Kevin a questioning look, but his brother shook his head. "I need somethin' stronger, don't you?"

Mike set up three shot glasses and poured out some expensive, little-used brandy. Kevin lifted his glass. "For Free Ireland." They tossed down the brandy and slammed the shot glasses onto the bar. "For Free Ireland."

The tavern wouldn't open for another three hours, so Kevin went off to bed and Mike and Bud sat in silence, nursing another brandy. Finally, Bud began setting up the bar. When someone knocked at the front door, his heart stuttered. After a long minute he peeked out to see Rose, and unlocked the door.

She threw her arms around him and looked up into his face. "Are you all right? I wanted to make sure you weren't hurt."

"I'm fine, Rose. How are your brothers?"

"They said the ambush was awful."

He swallowed. "I saw lots worse in the trenches in France, but some of Joe's crew had never killed anyone before."

Rose bit her lip. "Maybe now you'll be thinkin' about goin' to America."

He gave her a long look. "Now's not the time to make

such a decision, Rose."

She nodded. "Can you talk about it? The ambush, I mean?"

Bud looked up at the ceiling for a long minute. "It wasn't pretty, Rose. But we got the job done. Now the Tans know that vengeance doesn't belong just to the English."

"Everyone is talkin' about what you did. They're all excited. The Mayo Times even sold out their edition of the paper this morning. One article that described what you did called it 'retribution to the English'."

Bud nodded. "'Retribution' sounds so clean. Killin' men is anything but clean."

"What do you think will happen now?" she asked.

"I think ..." He hesitated. "I think more people are goin' to get involved, and things are going to get more violent. I think we have to be prepared for more fightin'. And I think more people are goin' to get killed."

Chapter Eleven

Different Directions

A week later, Joe Ring called another meeting at his farmhouse, and once more as Bud took a seat next to Maggie and Rose, he found himself apprehensive. Then he noticed two fair-haired men and an older woman he didn't recognize talking with a dark-haired couple. *Never saw any of those folks before. Maybe Walter knows who they are.* But at his inquiring glance, Walter shook his head.

Rose leaned toward him. "What is this meetin' all about?"

"I don't know," he whispered. "But there are some new people here." He tipped his head toward the back of the room where the strangers sat.

Conversation finally died down, and Joe Ring opened the meeting. "I just returned from Dublin," he announced. "I met with Eamon de Valera and Cathal Brugha, the Minister of Defense, and I reported what we're doing here in Westport. We have the attention of the Irish nation, and since the Mills family killin', a number of people want to join us. We cannot invite others until we vet them, but now I'd like to introduce some new members that we trust."

He paused and tipped his head toward the strangers. "I'd like you to meet Jerry and Mary Veronica Flatley and the Shannon's, Brian and Mary Pat." He paused and surveyed the room. "And you all remember Mike McGwire. He's back from America, where he's been raisin' money for us. He'll be going back after this meetin' tonight."

"Tell us more about your meetin' with de Valera," someone called.

"Right. They're excited about what we're accomplishin' up here, and they said they would support whatever we try to do. The Dail has started swearin' in Republican judges. That means County Mayo will have a Republican judge assigned to it. In the meantime, we should boycott the British courts. Don't use them. If you have a legal problem, take it up with a Republican circuit judge. The new judges will interpret laws passed by our Dail. And," he continued with a smile, "Minister of Defense Cathal Brugha is organizin' the new Irish Republican Police, so if you need police assistance, call the IRP, not the English constables. We want to put the English constables out of business, too."

"How do we get in touch with the Irish Republican Police?" one of the newcomers asked.

"We'll let you know how to contact them when they're in place here. They need new recruits, preferably from groups like ours. They'll go to Dublin for a week's trainin' and then return to Westport."

"And how are the constables and the Tans goin' to react to these new police?" Alan Ludden asked.

Joe frowned. "Not well, I suspect. We should expect resistance. How *much* resistance, I don't know."

"Where would a man sign up?" Alan asked.

Rose put her hand on Bud's arm. "You've been looking for a job," she whispered. "And you have military training. Maybe you should consider this new police force."

"Maybe," Bud said. "I'll talk to Joe after the meetin'."

She squeezed his hand.

Joe Gill jerked to his feet. "Come on, Joe. Do you really think this is goin' to work? We're makin' progress with our fight. Now we just lay down, and the English go away because we have some judges roamin' around? That's not goin' to work, Joe. The only thing the English understand is violence."

"Cathal Brugha agrees with you," Ring responded. "But he says if we do anythin' that's not directly tied to some atrocity committed by the Tans or the constables, we could lose public support. We have to be careful when we act. We can boycott without bein' violent."

He stopped and caught Rose's eye. "So, ladies, de Valera wants us to boycott all English businesses. That means you avoid buyin' your groceries and such from Protestant stores and you refuse service to Protestant customers. And you men, talk to the Irish Catholic deputy constables about joining the IRP police."

"I disagree," Joe Walsh shouted, heaving his bulky frame out of his chair. "We need to do more."

After a pause, Ring nodded. "All right, I hear you. Along with usin' our judges and police, maybe we take a different direction. The tax collector offices are closed after the business day is over, so maybe we burn 'em to the ground. That will disrupt their ability to collect taxes or even know who's paid and who hasn't."

"What else can we do?" Rose called suddenly.

Bud poked an elbow into her ribs. He sure didn't want Rose involved in anything that might get violent.

"What else?" Ring echoed. "How about this. The constables have small lightly armed stations in the countryside, and some of them are occupied by the Black and Tans. I say we attack them, seize their guns, and burn down the barracks."

Bud shut his eyes as those assembled murmured their approval. *Doesn't Joe Ring realize these things could get more people killed?*

"What do we do about the Tans or constables manning the barracks?" a man called.

Bud's lids snapped open when Ring began to speak.

"We draw them away," Joe responded. "For example, there's a small station in Ballintubber, in south central Mayo. It's a two-man substation, and they close about twelve midnight. Let's say we go over an hour after they close, break in, steal their firearms, and then set it on fire."

Another, louder murmur ran around the room.

"We keep that up," Ring said with a grin, "and the Tans and constables will hesitate to leave the city limits."

"Do you want volunteers?" young Tim Keough asked.

Joe nodded. "I have some men in mind for the Ballintubber operation. If you're interested in joinin' our new police force, see me after the meetin'."

Bud turned to Rose. "What do you think? Should I join Joe Ring's new force?"

She touched his arm. "I would be so proud if you did," she whispered. "But I'm worried about trouble. I don't want you to get hurt."

"It's right to be cautious," he whispered. "I'm not sure about a renegade police force that's in uniform. That's like wearin' a target on your back. I'll give it a few weeks to see how it works out."

Ring motioned to him and pulled him aside. "Are you interested in goin' to Ballintubber after the police barracks closes on Friday?"

Bud hesitated. "Who else is going?"

"I want you, Alan Ludden, Joe Gill, and Joe Walsh. Maybe Tim Keough, too. He wants to prove himself after upchuckin' at the ambush."

He thought for a minute. "All right, I'm in."

After the meeting broke up, they were joined outside by Rose's youngest brother, Terry Ludden. "I signed up for that new police force, the IRP," Terry announced. "I'm leavin' for training in Dublin next Monday."

* * *

The tavern was busy Friday night, but Bud managed to steal time away from the bar to ready the weapons for the six men going to Ballintubber. He got the revolvers out of the hidden cache, stuffed them in a burlap sack, and left them in the back of the tavern. When he returned to the bar, four men were ordering beer. Mike served them, and Bud went to answer a knock at the back door. It was Joe Walsh.

Walsh swept up the burlap bag and jumped in the waiting car. Bud followed, then passed out the pistols. The drive to Ballintubber took less than 30 minutes.

Joe Ring was already there. "Bud Ryan and Tim Keough," Ring called. "I want the two of you to keep an eye out."

Bud nodded, and he and young Keogh separated from the others and spread out. Bud pulled out his Bulldog and studied the area around the barracks. As expected, the rural police station was dark, and Joe Gill and Joe Walsh took sledgehammers to the barracks front door.

Suddenly a dark shadow appeared. "What's going on here?" a man shouted.

Tim Keough spun around and fired. The shot surprised Bud, and he leveled his revolver in the direction of the sound. He saw a dark figure drop to the ground.

Oh, God, what had the kid done?

Ring raced over and pressed Keough's gun hand down. "What the hell are you doing?"

At that moment the downed man, apparently uninjured, leaped to his feet and fled into the darkness.

"Tim," Ring spat, "did you even see his face before blastin' away?"

"I'm ... I'm sorry."

Alan Ludden joined them. "Did you recognize him? That was Deputy Constable Morgan."

Ring asked, "Did he recognize you, Alan?"

"I don't know."

"Tim?"

"I don't know," Keough replied. "I don't know if he even knows me."

Bud gritted his teeth. *This is going to end in more trouble.*

Ring ran his fingers through his hair. "This is exactly what I want to avoid! Come on, mates. Now we'll have to finish the job before Constable Morgan returns with some friends."

Walsh and Joe Gill went back to work on the door, and when it caved in, Bud and Alan Ludden slipped inside, emptied two gasoline containers on the floor and the counters and splashed more on the walls. Ring found a small cache of rifles, loaded them into his car, and then retreated. Joe Gill lit a match and tossed it in.

The interior of the police station ignited with a loud swoosh, and the men piled into their cars and headed back to Westport. "Alan," Ring said as they drove, "I'd stay around your farm for a couple of days while we see if anything develops from this."

"Will do."

They dropped Bud behind the tavern. He let himself in and stashed the burlap bag of guns in the cellar. Then he came upstairs, tied on his apron, and filled bar orders. When the last patrons left, Mike locked the front door and turned to him.

"How did it go?"

"We burned down the barracks like we planned, but Deputy Constable Morgan surprised us. Tim Keough wasn't thinkin' and shot at him."

"Bad news, that. Was Morgan hurt?"

"Don't know. He jumped up and ran off. We think he may have got a good look at Alan Ludden or Tim, but we don't know if he recognized them."

"That's bad luck for certain," Mike breathed.

The following morning Bud slept late, then decided to go out for a walk. At the police station, just down the street, the armored car sat idling at the front entrance, and several Tans were milling around. Two more Tans were lugging the Jennings machine gun from the station and loading it into the squad car along with a couple of belts of cartridges.

Bud's stomach clenched, but he strolled up and asked, "What's going on?"

One of the Tans looked over his shoulder. "Get away from me, mick," he muttered. "There's bad business about."

Chapter Twelve

More Killing

Bud watched the Tan captain cup his hands around his mouth. "All right, let's move out," he yelled. He expected them to head toward Ballintubber, but instead the armored vehicle, followed by the squad car full of Tans, drove off in a different direction. With a sick feeling, he realized they could be heading in the direction of the Ludden farm. *Lord God in heaven, that means the Luddens could be in mortal danger.*

A thousand thoughts raced through his mind. *Oh, Jesus, no. Not Rose's family. Please God, let them be going somewhere else.*

He raced back to the tavern and pounded up the stairs

just as Mike was coming down. "Do me a favor, Mike," Bud panted, terror in his voice. "Tell Joe Ring I'm not sure where the Tans are going, but they loaded the Jennings into the squad car, then both it and the armored car headed in the direction of the Ludden farm."

Mike sucked in his breath. "I'll tell him. What are you goin' to do?"

Bud didn't answer. He was already pounding up the stairs. He stepped into his room, slipped his hands behind his dresser, and retrieved his Bulldog. Then, he raced down the stairs, out the back door, and ran for Keough Stables to get a horse.

He rode hard. Just as he neared the Ludden farm, he heard the unmistakable rat-tat-tat of a machine gun. He reined up short and froze. *God damn it. All right, Sergeant Ryan, what would a sensible military officer do now?*

He headed into a stand of birch trees, slid off the horse, and tethered the lathered animal to a tree limb. Very quietly he worked his way around to the trees by the side of the house. *I'd give anything to have my platoon with me now.*

Then he saw two bodies lying face down in the front yard. *Oh my God. Oh my God.* He pulled out his revolver and waited, his mind racing. He wanted revenge, but getting himself killed was not going to help.

He couldn't make out who was on the ground, but from

the trees he watched four Tans with rifles open fire on the house. Two more Tans circled behind the house. *Maybe I can get those two while they're are out of sight of the others.* Immediately he rejected that idea. The others would hear it, and then he'd be caught in a shootout.

After a long, silent minute, Alan Ludden suddenly bolted from the front door, firing a shotgun at the machine gun crew. Bud watched in horror as the riflemen cut him down.

Without thinking he started forward, then thought better of it. He aimed his Bulldog at the closest man but knew he shouldn't fire. He would be no match for a Jennings and six riflemen. Never in his life had he felt so helpless. This was worse than France.

One of the Tans warily approached Alan, rolled him over with his foot, and felt for a pulse. After a moment he straightened. "We got him!"

The bastards. Oh, Lord, where are Rose and Maggie?

Smoke began billowing from the farmhouse roof, and all at once he realized the Tans had set the house on fire. He froze. *Rose! Was she inside?*

Flames ate into the structure as the Tans milled around, looking for more occupants. One walked within an arm's length of Bud but didn't see him. *I could rip his throat out.*

Two of the Tans broke in the front door, and then he

heard a woman's scream. Bud started from his hiding place, then heard more shots followed by silence. In the next moment the Tans walked out of the house and waved. "We got them all."

A blind haze of hate clouded his vision. They killed Rose and Maggie! He swallowed down a bitter taste in his mouth. *They will pay for this.*

He could do nothing but watch as the house burned while the Tans disassembled the Jennings and loaded it back into the squad car. The instant they drove off, Bud bolted out of the woods, shouting for Rose. In the front yard, he paused to kneel by the bodies for a few seconds. Terry Ludden and his father were both dead. Alan lay sprawled face up, but he wasn't breathing. The front of the house was perforated by two rows of machine gun bullets.

When he heard a faint voice, he lifted his head, then raced for the front door. "Rose?"

"Bud?" came an unsteady voice. "Bud, is that you?"

He ripped the front door off its hinges, and Rose stepped out of the house. His knees threatened to buckle when he saw her. Blood stained one of her sleeves, and she had her other arm wrapped around Maggie, who was coughing convulsively. He stepped forward and slid one arm about her waist.

"She breathed in a lot of smoke," Rose said in a shaky

voice. "I don't see any blood on her."

He started for the front door. "Is there anyone else in the house?"

She shook her head. Her eyes looked odd, unfocused. "Only M-Mom, but she's ... she's dead. They found her in the kitchen and sh-shot her."

Bud tried to see into the house. "Are you sure she's not just wounded?" He took a single step inside the front door just as the roof caved in, sending burning embers swirling into the air. Rose made a strangled sound and turned away.

In the next instant, a car drove into the yard, and Joe Ring and his brothers tumbled out, all brandishing firearms. Walter's face had gone dead white, and without saying a word he went to Maggie and wrapped his arms around her.

Bud cradled a shaking, sobbing Rose, holding her bleeding arm away from her body. "How bad are you hurt?" he asked gently.

"Not too bad," she said unsteadily. "One of the machine gun bullets clipped me."

Bud stripped off his shirt and wet it at the well pump, ripped open Rose's sleeve, and cleaned the wound.

"What happened?" Joe asked in a strained voice.

Bud told them, and admitted his frustration at being outnumbered so he couldn't attack.

Joe frowned. "If you'd even tried it, man, you'd be dead,

too. Now you can help us strike back at these devils."

Cradling a shotgun, Joe studied the bodies in the front yard for a long minute, then stalked around the entire perimeter of the still-burning structure, shaking his head.

"Jesus," he breathed when he returned. "Jesus Christ and all the saints. How could they? *How could they?*"

"Rose, can you tell me what happened?" he asked.

She released a long breath. "Like Bud said, the armored car and the squad car rolled up to the house and parked. Th-they took out the machine gun and assembled it while we watched from the front window. We didn't really know what they were d-doin' until they pointed it at the house and started firing."

She stopped and swallowed. "Dad and Terry went out, but ..." She swallowed hard and looked away. "Maggie and I ran to the back of the house and hid under the mattress on her bed. One of the machine gun bullets went r-right through it and hit my arm."

Maggie stopped coughing and took a deep breath of fresh air. "One of the Tans shouted out that Alan was under arrest. Alan yelled back that he wasn't comin' out, and they started firin' into the house again."

Rose laid her hand on her sister's arm. "Dad and Terry went outside to talk to them." She swallowed again. "The Tans s-shot them both. Then the shootin' stopped, and when it was quiet for some time Alan made a break for it."

Bud felt sick. He nodded, his jaw clenched. "What about your mom?"

Rose looked off in the distance for a long moment. "We heard someone break in, and then we heard Mom scream. I'll never forget that scream. Never." She swiped tears off her cheek.

"Rose," Bud said, "Rose, don't."

"I'm all right," she said dully. "They searched the house, but they didn't find us. Then the upstairs rooms filled with smoke, and it got so we couldn't breathe, so we stayed low and crawled to the window. We watched the ceiling catch fire, so we moved as close as we could to the front door, but we didn't dare go outside. Then I heard Bud's voice."

Holding tight to Walter, Maggie started toward the men lying in the yard. Walter rolled one over, then another. Terry and their father. Maggie fell to her knees and wrapped both arms across her midriff. Rose stood rigid, staring down at her brother and her father, and then Alan.

"I can't cry," she whispered, her voice hoarse. "It hurts too much to cry."

Joe Ring touched her shoulder. "We're goin' to have to keep you and Maggie hidden."

"Hidden where?"

Joe sent Bud a look. "In the cellar room at Ryan's

tavern."

Bud nodded. "Joe, I came out on Tim Keough's horse. Could you get it back to his stable?"

"Sure. No bother."

Joe drove to the tavern, where Bud unlocked the back door and escorted everyone into the hidden room in the cellar. Then he took Joe aside. "Get Dr. Reilly. Tell him what happened and ask him to come and stitch up Rose's arm."

Joe nodded and left without a word. As the door closed behind him, Mike appeared on the cellar stairs. "Lord Jesus, what's happened? I was getting' ready to open the tavern when I heard a lot of noise in the street. The Tans were shoutin' about something, sounded like they were celebrating. So, I went down the street to see what it was all about. Nobody could tell me anythin'."

Bud took a deep breath and explained about the attack on the Luddens, then climbed the stairs to the tavern to make something for the girls and Walter to eat. As he sliced bread for sandwiches and brewed a pot of strong tea, he found himself feeling strangely calm. Some kind of shock, probably. But as he sliced up a ripe tomato, he thought about taking revenge for the Ludden killings. And the more he thought about it, the more sense it made.

When Joe Ring returned with Dr. Reilly, Bud took him aside. "Joe, could you get enough military grade explosives to blow up a small bridge?"

Joe frowned. "Bud, what are you thinkin'?"

"I'm thinkin' I want to blow up the Tan's armored car."

"Whisht, man, that's won't be easy. Do you want to blow it up behind the police station?"

"Not behind the station. I want to blow it up when it's full of Tans. There's no way we can attack the armored car straight on, but if we could lure it across a bridge loaded with dynamite, I could rig it so when the bridge blows, the armored car will slide off into the water below. Some place over a river deep enough so the car falls in, the interior fills with water."

Joe looked at him sharply. "You sure about this, Bud?"

"I'm sure. We have enough men to kill any Tans that don't drown in the car."

"What about the squad car? It usually follows the armored car. What do we do about that?"

"We ambush the squad car when the armored car falls into the river."

Joe thought for a moment. "I think I know where to get the explosives."

"Then get them," Bud said. "Soon."

* * *

Three days later, as Bud was eating breakfast, Mike burst into the tavern and threw the morning edition of the Mayo News onto the counter. "The Tans have gone completely off the rails," he spat.

Bud looked up from his oatmeal. "What now?"

"They're no longer satisfied with raidin' isolated farmhouses and killin' people. Now they're attackin' whole towns. They sacked Balbriggan and Trim outside of Dublin, and Tralee in southern Ireland. Just burned everything to the ground."

Bud scanned the front page of the newspaper, then tossed it aside. "I need to see Joe Ring."

"Why? How's that going to save a town?"

"Because yesterday mornin' I found somethin' Joe and I talked about yesterday. An ambush site."

Mike stared at him. "Ambush? Are you daft?"

"Maybe. Just outside of Blackharbor, there's a bridge over the Paulee River."

Mike said nothing, just frowned and sipped his tea.

That afternoon, Bud wheeled his bicycle out of the shed and pedaled out to the Ring farm. "Joe, have you seen the morning paper?"

He nodded. "I have. The Tans are runnin' wild."

"Not for long," Bud said. "I know where we can ambush that damned armored car."

Chapter Thirteen

Counterstrike

A day later, Bud laid his bicycle against the Ring farmhouse porch and looked up to see a shirtless Joe Ring wave him in out of the cold morning air and into the warmth of the kitchen. The ride from Westport in the spring drizzle had chilled him through his jacket and shirt.

He hesitated. "Where are Jack and Walter?"

"Didn't you see them on the hill behind the farm?"

"I didn't see anyone."

"It's probably good you didn't. They're hidden, watchin' for Tans. So, sit down and let me get a shirt on. Maybe make us some tea while you wait."

Bud watched him retreat into the back of the house, then

filled the teakettle at the kitchen pump and set it on the stove. After he found a ceramic teapot, he sat down to wait.

When Joe returned, he startled Bud with a question. "What you have come up with?"

Bud sucked in a breath. "There's a town in south County Mayo. Blackharbor. You know it?"

"I know it. We burned down the police station a few weeks ago. Now there's not much left other than a tax collection office, a pub, and a general store. Maybe a few houses scattered along what passes for the main street." He set out two cups and a canister of tea.

"The Paulee River runs along the north edge of town," Bud said. "There's a wooden bridge that leads into town. It's an old bridge, just wide enough for a single vehicle. No walkway, no guardrail. If a car was stopped on the bridge there'd be no room for anybody to step out of it."

The teakettle whistled, and Joe dumped a small handful of tea leaves into the ceramic pot. "Yeah, I remember that bridge. It's narrow and rickety. You have to go slow to keep from drivin' off the edge."

"I can set explosives on the west supports of the bridge," Bud explained. "When they detonate, any car on the bridge will pitch into the river."

"How many Tans do you think there will be in a vehicle?" Joe interrupted, splashing hot tea into Bud's cup.

"Maybe six in the armored car, and another six or eight in that squad car that goes out with it. It could be as many as fourteen Tans, I'm guessin'."

Joe leaned back in his chair and rubbed his chin. "Our column doesn't have enough men for this big a mission, and I don't want to take any chances. The southern Westport IRA operates in that area. I'll contact them and set up a joint operation."

"When will the dynamite be available?"

"Dave Gallaher says he has a source for explosives, but I haven't heard back from him."

"It has to be military grade, Joe. Not industrial grade. And tell him not to forget the detonator."

"Anythin' else?"

Bud hesitated. "Well, yes. The Ludden girls should be there."

Joe frowned. "Don't you think that would be dangerous?"

"We should let them come. They lost their entire family because of the Tans. Killin' Tans will feel justified to them."

"All right," Joe said slowly. "But you're responsible for them."

* * *

Back at the tavern, Bud tried to keep his thoughts off the Paulee River bridge, but he couldn't help turning the plan over and over in his mind. Around five o'clock, Deputy Constable Harris and another uniformed deputy constable walked in. Bud stared at them for a long minute, then pointed to the door. "Out," he shouted. "You're not welcome here."

Constable Harris blinked. "Hold on, Ryan. We're looking for Rose and Maggie Ludden. We want to talk to them."

Bud faced them and propped his hands on his hips. "You want to see the Ludden sisters, do you? Well, about this time of day they'd be home cookin' supper for their family, except that ..." He leaned across the bar. "Your damned Tans murdered their family and burned their house to the ground. They're not likely to speak to you."

Constable Harris stepped back. "Jesus, Ryan, that wasn't us."

Bud raised his voice. "The Tans are deputy constables. They work for you." Again, he pointed to the door. "Out."

"Ah, be reasonable, mate. We're investigating what happened at the Luddens that day, and we need to talk to Rose and Maggie about it."

Bud reached under the bar for the shotgun. "Go ask your Tan mates." He aimed the gun at the constable's chest.

Constable Harris lifted his hands in the air and pivoted toward the door, then did an about-face and tipped his chin toward the shotgun. "You know I could arrest you for pointing that gun at me."

Bud raised the shotgun an inch. "Come and take it."

"Look, the fact is the Tans went out to the Ludden farm to talk to Alan Ludden about Ballintubber. They said Alan came out of the house shooting at them, and there were other shooters in the house as well. The Tans did what they had to do."

Bud lowered the shotgun. "The fact is," he said slowly, "they're lyin'."

"How do you know that?"

"Because I was there. I saw it all."

Harris said nothing.

"What about the Mills family?" Bud continued.

"Rick Mills was a suspected IRA agent."

"So why kill Rick's wife and their four-year-old daughter? You think little Ashlyn was IRA, too?" He raised the shotgun again. "Out, Constable. Get out of our tavern and don't come back."

"Ah, Bud, be reasonable, man. We've been mates for a long while. We have to find a way to work this out."

Bud came out from behind the bar. "It's too late for that, Constable. Go back to England and leave the Tans to us."

Using the barrel of the shotgun, he shoved both men out the door just as Kevin appeared from upstairs.

"What's all the shoutin' about?"

Bud stowed the shotgun back under the bar. "Constable Harris and his partner were here lookin' for Rose and Maggie. I threw them out."

Kevin joined Mike behind the bar. "We have to get along with the constables, Bud. The English sent the Tans. At some point they'll call them back, but the constables will stay."

"Not likely," Bud shot back. "The constables have to go, too."

Both brothers stared at him. "De Valera and Brugha are right," Bud added. "We can't work with the constables. We need to drive them all out, have our own police."

Mike and Kevin looked at each other without speaking.

"Watch the bar," Bud said. "I need to go downstairs and cool off." On his way down to the cellar he knocked on the wall to alert the girls.

"Rose, it's me."

"What was all the shoutin' upstairs?"

"Deputy Constable Harris and another deputy came lookin' for you and Maggie. They wanted to question you about the shootin' at your farm."

Rose turned pale. "What do you think we should do?"

Bud thought for a moment. "Nothin'. We're past workin'

with them. I used to think maybe we could find some middle ground, but after that day at your farm, all I want to do is kill Tans."

"Oh, Bud, you can't mean that," Rose said with anger in her voice.

"I do mean it. We're goin' to ambush them on the bridge over the Paulee River."

Rose squeezed her hands into fists and sent him a long, steady look. "Then Maggie and I want to be there. You're doin' this because the Tans killed our family, and the Mills family, too. Maggie and I have earned the right to watch any retribution we take."

Bud nodded agreement, then looked away.

* * *

The next morning, Kevin bounded into Bud's bedroom before he was fully awake. "England has proposed a treaty!" he chortled.

Bud shook himself awake. "What? What are you talkin' about?"

"England has offered us a Republic! But," he added, "there are conditions."

Bud's elation evaporated. Oh, damn. Here it comes. "What conditions?"

"First, they want a ceasefire. Then Ireland gets partitioned into a Republic, which includes all of the south and three counties in Ulster. The other six Ulster counties stay with the United Kingdom."

"Leave it to the politicians to muck it up," Bud muttered. Nevertheless, he climbed out of bed, pulled on trousers and a sweater, and tramped down to the cellar to give Rose and Maggie the news.

Rose threw her arms around him. "This is wonderful, Bud! We should be celebratin'."

"I don't think so. We're still goin' ahead with the Paulee River bridge plan."

Kevin appeared in the doorway. "We should expect a big crowd celebratin' at the tavern today, Bud. Bring up a few extra cases of whiskey and another of beer."

They opened the tavern early, and customers began to pour in. In the middle of the celebration, Walter Ring arrived and took Bud aside. "Joe says he's got the explosives. Tell Kevin, Mike, and the girls to be at our farm tomorrow mornin' at eleven to make final plans."

Bud clenched his teeth. *Final plans.* A whole meeting with everybody? The Blackharbor plan had to be kept secret, so why risk someone blabbing to the Tans?

* * *

The next morning Joe Gill circled his Renault around the hill to the Ring farm. He parked it, and Rose, Maggie, Mike, Kevin, Bud, and Gill's wife, Brigit, all squeezed out of the car. The already assembled crowd was too large to fit in the house, so Joe Ring moved a table and some chairs into the farmyard. Bud didn't recognize some of the people, and that made him nervous.

"All right, everybody, let's get this meetin' started," Joe called. "First, I'd like to introduce Patrick Burke, head of the southern Westport Flying Column."

A tall, imposing man with red hair and a generous mustache stood up and waved. He wore a cap tilted at a jaunty angle.

"And you all know Rose and Maggie Ludden," Joe continued. "The Blackharbor operation will be payback for the attack on the Ludden home and the one that killed the Mills family."

Rose leaned toward Bud. "It's heartenin' that so many people want to make what happened right," she whispered.

Bud said nothing. There was no way to "make anything right" as long as the Tans were free to kill the Irish.

"We're here to plan an attack on the Tans at Blackharbor," Ring continued.

An older, overweight man on Bud's left stood up. "The

English have offered a treaty," he shouted. "If we go ahead with this operation, are we goin' to make a hash of any treaty negotiations?"

Ring thought for a moment. "If we back off," he said at last, "the treaty negotiations will be extended. If there's no fightin', there's no reason for the treaty, now is there? Negotiations will go on and on and will never be made final. If we bloody up the Tans, that gives them a reason for a ceasefire and a reason to make a treaty in our favor. Don't you see, mates? We have to earn our country back."

A murmur ran through the crowd.

"Now," Joe continued, "about the operation. Bud Ryan will explain the Blackharbor plan."

Bud stood up and explained the general plan for the bridge ambush.

When he finished, Patrick Burke tilted his head. "The squad car always follows that armored vehicle, right? What about the Tans ridin' in that?"

"We shoot them," Bud said quietly.

A sudden silence settled over the crowd. Then someone shouted another question. "When are we goin' to do this?"

"The day after tomorrow," Joe Ring answered. "We want the ladies to start a rumor that the IRA will be meetin' in Blackharbor at eleven o'clock that morning to discuss the ceasefire and the treaty. That will draw the Tans out of

Westport."

The people at the meeting looked at one another and nodded.

Joe continued. "Bud, I want you to coordinate with Pat Burke. He knows the area well. Lay out where you want his marksmen deployed."

Another silence. Finally, Joe raised his arm. "Afterward, we'll need to get the Blackharbor residents out of the area. The Tans will almost certainly launch an attack against the town, and they'll kill anyone they find."

"What do we do with the residents?" a man shouted.

"Ah, that," Ring said. "We send them to America."

"All of them?"

"All of them."

When the meeting finally broke up, Bud found his hands balled into fists. *The Tans need to die. They want war; we're giving them war.*

The morning of the operation, Bud got up early and went down to the cellar. Rose and Maggie were already up and dressed.

"I don't think it's a good idea to take you girls with us," Bud said slowly. "Are you sure you want to watch this?"

"We're sure," Rose said, her mouth unsmiling. "If this is the only way we're going to drive the Tans out of Ireland, we want to be there."

Bud looked down at her, thinking how much he loved her, how much he admired her. He gave her a peck on the cheek.

Then they all piled into Joe Gill's car and headed south to Blackharbor.

Chapter Fourteen

Blackharbor

The sun had broken over the horizon, but the early morning fog still lingered in the valleys. The Renault joined a caravan of cars, carriages, and horses along the Westport-Blackharbor Road where they congregated in the woods on the north bank of the Paulee River, out of sight. Bud climbed out of the car, carefully unloaded the explosives, and distributed the dynamite sticks to the men. He explained what he wanted them to do, and they trekked off onto the bridge to begin work. Rose and Maggie waited behind a brushy hillock.

The current below the bridge was swift, and Bud knew that if the armored car fell into the river, the Tans wouldn't have a chance. He looked to the west where a thunderstorm was gathering and called down to his crew, "Be sure to position the dynamite under the timbers so the rain won't wet it."

Their progress was slow and careful, but the wait made him nervous. *This is taking too long.* He checked the road to the north, half expecting to see the Tans' armored car rolling toward him, but the road was empty. Relieved, he paced up and down, occasionally kneeling to give instructions to the men working below.

Finally, he heard what he wanted to hear. "We're done down here," yelled one of the crew. "Do you want us to run the wires?"

"I'll set the wires myself. Come on up and get out of here."

When the last man climbed up onto the bridge, Bud carefully picked his way down to the wooden support structure and worked his way to the southern end of the bridge, unspooling wire as he went. He set the detonator behind a pile of boulders and laid the bare wires next to it, then secured the loose ends under a good-sized rock, ready to connect them just before the armored car drove onto the bridge.

"It's all set," he called to Joe Ring at the far end of the bridge. He repeated the message to Pat Burke, hidden in a ditch at the other end. Joe and Burke then directed the rebel squads into position to maximize the fields of fire from the woods bordering the north bank of the Paulee. When they were ready, Burke positioned a pair of marksmen in the brush on the southern side of the bridge in case any Tans tried to escape to the south bank. Joe's group settled in to ambush the squad car that would be trapped on the road in front of the damaged bridge.

Bud retreated to where Rose and Maggie crouched, their revolvers drawn. "Joe Gill's wife, Brigit, is a nurse. Where is she hidden?"

"In the woods on the north bank," Rose said. "Joe brought some medical supplies in case anyone gets hit." She scanned the town behind her. "After it's over, how are we goin' to get out of here?"

"There's a carriage waitin' at the end of the main street behind us. There's room for six. When this is finished, we'll head west to Louisburgh and then circle back to Westport."

He could smell rain in the air. He wasn't worried about the dynamite; he was more concerned about the wind. The prevailing breeze blew west to east, which would blow the smoke away and give the marksmen downriver a clear field of fire. He glanced up at the sky and prayed the rain would hold off for one more hour.

Suddenly a voice called out from the opposite bank.

"Here they come. Get into position."

Bud crouched behind the boulders with Rose and Maggie huddled close by, then stuck his head up to see two vehicles approaching the bridge. When they drew closer, he realized the squad car was in the lead. He swore under his breath.

"What's wrong?" Rose whispered.

"I didn't expect the squad car to be in the lead. We can't let it come onto the bridge and just wait there for the armored vehicle. That would put most of the Tans behind us, and their gunfire could cut us up."

"Then blow the bridge up now," Maggie said.

"I can't. That leaves only the marksmen on the other bank to attack the Tans in the armored car." His mind raced. The wind had shifted, and he noted it was now blowing the wrong direction. Then the first drops of rain began to fall.

God-Jesus-and-all-the-saints, what do I do now?"

He connected the wires to the detonator, but then hesitated and pulled the detonator's plunger up into a neutral position.

The squad car slowed down as it drove onto the bridge, and suddenly Maggie bolted out of their hiding place and ran toward the vehicle.

Bud froze. "Maggie, don't!" he yelled.

But she didn't stop. She trotted ten feet onto the bridge,

stood in front of the squad car, and cupped her hands around her mouth. "Hey," she shouted. "Are you looking for me?"

What the hell is she doing? He lifted his hands off the detonator.

Both squad car front doors opened, and two Tans stepped out onto the running board. The driver yelled, "Get out of the way! Get off the bridge!"

The armored car caught up and slowed behind it.

"I came to surrender," Maggie yelled.

"Get off the bridge, you daft bitch! We need to get into town."

"You're not going anywhere until I say you are," she screamed.

The armored vehicle crept closer, swung the turret on top of the car, and aimed it at Maggie. She crouched down in front of the squad car so the turret operator couldn't see her.

"You bastards killed my family!" she screamed.

"Maggie Ludden," one of the Tans called. "Is that you? You're under arrest." He reached for his service revolver and leveled it at her.

Unexpectedly, she stood up and shouted a single word. "*Now!*"

Chapter Fifteen

Mis-Steps

Bud crossed himself and pushed the plunger.

The blast threw Maggie into the air and onto her back, and Bud's entire body went cold. He drew his Bulldog and raced toward her prone body. The bridge buckled, and a cloud of white smoke obscured the left side of the bridge, and then both vehicles began to slide sideways into the river.

Maggie lay without moving. One Tan fired his revolver at her but missed. Bud fired his revolver and dropped to his knee, then glimpsed Rose racing toward him, firing her pistol. Maggie rolled onto her stomach and started shooting until her revolver was empty.

Both the squad car and the armored car tumbled into

the river, and Bud and Rose kept firing at it. The Republican marksmen gathered on both banks, pouring gunfire into both vehicles. Some of the Tans struggled out of their vehicle and tried to swim to shore. They were shot, and the swift current carried the inert bodies downriver. Gunmen trotted alongside the bank and kept firing at them.

Bud and Rose ran to Maggie. She rolled over, face up, blinking her eyes.

"Are you daft?" Rose screamed at her sister. "You could have been killed!"

"Maggie," Bud yelled. "What's the matter with you?"

Maggie tried to smile. "Did we get them?"

Bud helped her sit up. "We got them. Are you hurt?"

"What?" she shouted. "I can't hear you."

Bud ran his hands over her. Her dress was torn and bloody, but she could move her arms and legs. She began to pick small pieces of wood out of the wounds on her body. "I think I'm all right," she said loudly.

They helped her to her feet, and the three of them stood on what was left of the bridge and looked downriver. The squad car's front bumper and headlights were all that was above water. The armored car was completely submerged.

"Rose, how are you feeling?" Bud asked.

"Strange. A little disappointed. I thought I would feel...happy. They deserved it, though."

"What did you say," Maggie shouted.

Bud looked over at her. "We need to get you out of here," he yelled. "Can you walk?"

"I think so," she hollered back.

He disconnected the wires from the detonator, then returned to Rose and Maggie and took one of Maggie's arms. Rose took the other, and then the three of them slowly made their way away from the bridge and down Blackharbor's main street. On the way, Pat Burke and two marksmen returned from the river bank and helped to lift Maggie into the waiting carriage.

"How did it go on the banks?" asked Bud.

"We got all we could see," Burke responded. "I don't think any of them made it out of the river alive. Some were still thrashin' around in the water, but the boys farther down took care of them. Ready to go?"

"We're ready," Bud said. "Do any of you have a loaded gun? All three of us are out of ammunition, and I don't want an escaped Tan jumpin' out of the woods at us."

Both marksmen told them not to worry. Burke then snapped the reins, and the carriage started moving.

Bud wrapped his arm around Rose and whispered in her ear. "I don't like takin' you with us on missions. You could get shot, or do some daft thing like Maggie and not be so lucky." He squeezed her shoulder.

She nodded but said nothing.

Burke drove the horses along the riverfront road toward Louisburgh just as the rain increased.

"My ears are still ringing," Maggie shouted.

Bud checked her ears for bleeding. "I think your hearing should be fine in an hour or two."

Rose nodded and gripped her sister's hand. Bud noticed her cheeks were wet. "What's the matter?"

She tipped her chin toward the river. "All those young men we killed. Do you think they had families?"

He looked away to see bodies floating in the river. "This was the life they chose," he said in a quiet voice. *What we did was for the Luddens and the Mills family. And for Ireland. I pray the rest of the Tans will leave Ireland soon.*

Burke snapped his whip over the horses again, and they picked up the pace. Finally, Bud saw the outskirts of Louisburgh ahead, and they turned up the street toward the stone bridge spanning the Paulee. Residents on the bridge were peering down at the river, watching bodies float past. When the carriage passed over the bridge, the townspeople pointed at them in silence.

Burke slowed the horses to a trot, and at last they reached Westport and the back door of Ryan's tavern. Once safely inside the secret cellar room, Maggie stumbled to her cot and sat with her arms clasped across her midriff, rocking back and forth. Bud settled beside her.

"That was a daft thing to do," he scolded. "You could have been—" He couldn't finish the sentence.

Rose wrapped her arms around her sister. "Make me some tea," Maggie murmured. "Very strong tea."

Bud tramped upstairs and had just set the teakettle on the stove when his brothers Kevin and Mike strode in. Kevin immediately grabbed Bud's sleeve. "How's Maggie?"

"Mostly she's all right, but she's a bit shaken so I'm makin' her a cup of tea. She's downstairs with Rose."

At that moment Walter and Joe Ring barreled in the back door. "Is Maggie all right?" Walter shouted.

Bud nodded. "She's downstairs," he said. Without a word, Walter pivoted and clattered down the cellar stairs.

Bud lifted the teapot off the kitchen shelf and added a double handful of black tea leaves. "Joe, after the dynamite went off, I didn't see much. How many Tans did we get?"

"A lot. I don't think we got them all, though. I saw some swimmin' in the river tryin' to escape."

When the tea had steeped, Bud poured out a cup for Maggie and set it on a tray with a slice of bread and butter. Then he and Joe descended to the cellar.

Walter was anxiously patting Maggie's slim frame all over while she tried to bat his hands away. "Walter, I'm not hurt. Stop manhandlin' me!"

He sank down beside her on the cot and ran his hands through his hair. "Maggie, what were you thinkin' to do a daft thing like that?"

Bud handed her the tray, and she sent him a shaky smile. "I wasn't thinkin'," she confessed. "I could see that the plan wouldn't work if that squad car blocked the way, so I ..."

She downed a swallow of tea.

Walter squeezed her shoulder, and she gave a tiny yelp.

"Oh, sorry," he said quickly. "Maggie, don't ever do anythin' like that again."

She nodded and bit into the slice of bread.

Joe Ring was pacing back and forth across the cellar, his head bent. After a short silence he met Bud's gaze. "Tomorrow mornin' we'll be havin' a meeting about the Kilmeena operation. Can you be there?"

"What's the Kilmeena operation?" Rose asked.

"Kilmeena's the backup plan we had if Blackharbor didn't go well. Now it's operational."

An awkward silence fell. "Rose, I wasn't going to tell you until after Blackharbor," Bud said. "You'll need to stay here with Maggie."

"Bud," Joe pressed, "can you be there?"

"I'll be there."

The next morning, he went down to the cellar to check

on Maggie. She was still asleep, but Rose was up and dressed. "I'm off to that meetin' out at Ring's farm," he said quietly. "I'll be sendin' Dr. Reilly along to check Maggie over. Will you stay with her?"

Rose squeezed his hand. "I will." She stretched up to kiss his cheek. "Don't volunteer for anythin'. Promise?"

He pulled her close. "I love you, Rose. You know that." When she nodded, he held her for a few seconds, then whispered, "I'll be back soon."

* * *

The meeting at the Ring farm turned out to be even bigger than the one three days ago. Bud counted over 50 people, with many faces he didn't recognize. *I'm not feeling good about this. Too many amateurs.*

He took a seat as Joe Ring stood up to speak. "The Irish Dail has just declared war on England. That means the Kilmeena operation is even more important."

"Explain it!" someone yelled.

"In a moment," Joe responded. "First, I have a word to say about the Westport and Castlebar columns and our success at Blackharbor. Twelve Tans were killed. Two of our members were slightly wounded, and one, Maggie Ludden, is still recovering." He scanned the crowd. "Bud Ryan, can you tell us how she's doin'?"

Bud stood up. "Maggie's doin' fine. Her hearing was affected, bein' so close to the blast, but she wasn't wounded."

"For those of you who weren't there," Joe continued, "Maggie Ludden ran from cover to stop the Tans vehicles on the Paulee River bridge. And that allowed us a safe hiding place to blow up the bridge with both the Tans' armored car and their squad car sittin' in the middle of it. And—" Joe shook his head. "Maggie was completely unarmed."

Bud jerked but kept silent. *Maggie was not unarmed. She emptied her revolver at the Tans. But I guess "unarmed" sounds better.*

The crowd murmured, then broke into spontaneous applause, and Bud smiled. He was proud of Maggie and of Rose as well. The pretty Ludden sisters were tougher than they looked.

When everyone quieted down, Joe turned to a tall man with a drooping red mustache wearing workmen's clothes. "I'm introducin' Michael Kilroy. Michael Collins has put him in charge of our Kilmeena operation. I'll be second in command, and we're unitin' three rebel columns for this action. From Westport, Brodie Malone will be in charge. From Castlebar, there's Dennis Flynn. And from Newport we have Jim Moran. Now Michael Kilroy is goin' to tell us about the plan."

The tall man rose and faced the crowd. "The Kilmeena police go about town well-armed, and their barracks are too well defended to attack head on. The constables and the Tans control the towns, but we control the countryside. So, we have to get the Kilmeena police out of their barracks and into the countryside."

"And just how do we do that?" a voice shouted.

Kilroy held up his hand. "I'll tell you how. Tomorrow night each of the three columns will stir up some trouble. Not in the town but outside, in the country. Come daylight that should bring the Kilmeena police out to reinforce the Westport, Newport, and Castlebar constables. They'll drive to the Westport-Newport Road and go either one direction or the other, so we set up an ambush at the intersection near the Knocknabola railroad bridge."

In the silence that followed Bud wondered why there were no questions.

When the meeting drew to a close, Bud walked over to short, stocky Brodie Malone and asked if he needed support for the Westport portion of the plan. "No, mate," Brodie said shortly. "We don't need help."

Bud blinked. He thought Brodie acted a bit aloof. *Something is wrong here.* He waited for Brodie to say more, then shrugged and headed back to Westport and the tavern, where he explained the Kilmeena plan to Kevin and Mike.

He left out the part about stirring up trouble in town tomorrow tonight. Whatever mischief Brodie Malone planned for the Westport rebels would suffice. Still, something about Brodie Malone kept nagging at him.

The next night Bud took the evening shift with Mike, and although the bar was busy, he heard no talk about anything out of the ordinary happening in town. That made him uneasy. *We should be hearing about some disruption or trouble, something to serve as a pretext for calling out the constables.*

At the end of a busy night they closed the tavern, and Bud visited briefly with Maggie and Rose before he went to bed. At dawn, he was to report to the Knocknabola Bridge.

He slept fitfully and had one of his old nightmares, but while it was still dark outside he got dressed, slipped his Bulldog into his pocket, and climbed into Joe Gill's Renault along with Kevin and Mike. They drove north and arrived at the bridge just after dawn. The command center was set up behind a brushy knoll, and the Renault headed for it. Bud rolled down his window to hear their orders.

"Take the right flank on the rise above the bridge," Joe Ring instructed. "Park the car up there behind the ridge, out of sight. If you can't get back to it, you can escape over the mountain to Skerdagh."

"Who else is with us on the flank?" Bud asked.

"Jim Moran and his Westport boys."

Gill climbed over the grassy hill overlooking the intersection of the Westport-Newport Road and the railroad bridge, his wheels spinning on the slippery, dew-drenched grass. Finally, they all piled out, unloaded the rifles and shotguns, and spread out along the ridge.

"How long before Brodie Malone and the Westport boys get here?" Bud asked.

Gill shrugged and stroked his mustache.

"How many of them are there?" Bud pursued.

"Should be somethin' like twenty mannin' each of the front lines."

The morning sun rose. As the spring day grew warmer, Bud watched another group of vehicles stop at the command center and speak with Joe Ring and Michael Kilroy.

Joe Gill stood up. "I'm going down there and see what's up." He made his way down the hill as vehicles were driven into the woods near the bridge and men began taking up positions on the opposite side. Bud watched Gill hold a short conference with Kilroy and Joe Ring and then hike back up to the ridge.

"What's going on?" he asked.

"Dennis Flynn and the Castlebar men didn't get anythin' unusual goin' last night, so there was no diversion at all. They said the police barracks were empty. All the constables must have been out on patrol, so the Castlebar men weren't able to shoot up the station."

All this planning and one group mucks it up? Don't tell me this is going to be a huge waste of time.

"Look," Mike said suddenly, pointing at the bridge. "Looks like the Newport mates are here."

Gill started down the hill, but Bud grabbed his arm. "I'll go." Despite his aching hip, he negotiated the descent in short order, walking up just as Jim Moran was reporting to Kilroy.

"We shot one of the constables as he was comin' out of the barracks," Moran said. "Paddy got him with his sniper rifle."

"How bad was he hurt?" Kilroy asked.

"Bullet through his temple. There's no way he survives that shot."

"That should bring the Kilmeena police out," Kilroy said. "Well done, Jim. Take your boys up the hill and spread out next to Bud Ryan and the rest of the men up there."

"Michael," Bud interrupted. "Has anybody heard from Brodie Moran and the rest of my Westport mates?"

"We've heard nothing so far. Why?"

Bud thought for a moment. "Without Brodie's bunch we're under-manned. Maybe we should call this off."

Kilroy glanced down the road and rubbed his chin. "We

have over forty men. That should give us a two-to-one advantage. Good odds to get the job done."

Bud shook his head, dissatisfied, but he turned away and climbed back up to his position on the ridge. He settled in next to his brother Mike, who leaned toward him. "What's going on?"

Bud told him. Mike then glanced up at the position of the sun. "This is taking too long. I'm walkin' back to Westport to open the tavern."

"What?"

"You heard me. We can't have the tavern closed without a good reason if a dozen or so constables get ambushed and killed. They're not stupid. If we don't open, they'll know we're involved." He handed his rifle to Bud and headed down the hill.

Bud looked over at Kevin and Joe Gill. "We can't man this ridge alone. I say we join the Castlebar boys."

They packed up and hiked over to the Castlebar line, explained the situation, and settled in next to their men. Bud watched the sun move directly over their heads in the cloudless sky and tried to tamp down his growing uneasiness.

Traffic between Westport and Newport was light. Hours passed, and finally he rolled over onto his back and lay in the warm sun, watching the clouds drift by overhead.

And then someone off to his left yelled, "Here they come!"

Chapter Sixteen

Kilmeena

All eyes turned to the road. Bud expected to see a squad car, but instead what appeared was a Chesley lorry, like the troop carriers the British had used in France. *Good. There will be more than six or seven constables in that lorry.* He sighted down his rifle barrel and aimed at the canvas covering over the back of the vehicle.

When it reached the intersection, the IRA men opened fire. The Tan driver and the constable in the passenger seat jumped out, and at that same moment the tailgate banged open and uniformed police poured onto the road. Crowding close to the lorry, they returned fire, spraying bullets into the woods and up on the ridge.

Bud emptied his rifle and had just reloaded when he spied another Chesley lorry racing toward the first one, followed by a squad car. This lorry swung wide of the road to form a protective barrier around the constables and the Tans on foot. He estimated there were now at least 30 men, all well-armed, firing on them from behind the vehicle barricade. He looked back at Joe Gill's Renault and thought about their escape route.

The constables organized themselves into three prongs and poured out from the safety of their vehicles. The section to Bud's right, just where the Westport column should have been positioned, advanced toward him.

"They're going to roll up on our flank!" he yelled to Dennis Flynn. Quickly he reorganized the men near him to defend themselves. In the next minute he noticed the constables' left section was charging into the woods, where they managed to force Jim Moran's group out of their protected hiding places. Moran's men retreated up the hill toward Bud's position.

By now the center prong of constables and Tans was directly assaulting the IRA firing line, advancing a few steps up the hill, then stopping to kneel and fire. After reloading, they pressed forward. *They're well-disciplined*, Bud thought. *More than that, they're lethal.*

"Fall back," he shouted. "Fall back!"

Joe Gill stood up to retreat, and a bullet caught him in the back. Bud ran to him, looped an arm around his shoulders, and walked him back toward his car. Two IRA men met them, and Bud let them take over.

As the front contracted, more Castlebar fighters fell back to Bud's position. Suddenly, one man pitched forward, blood from a head wound spattering onto his mates. Dragging their wounded with them, the Newport column retreated up the hill to join the Castlebar defensive line, and together they managed to halt the advance of constables and Tans. By this time, both groups were pouring bullets into each other's positions.

Bud stopped firing and tried to reassess their position. The mountain pass to Skerdagh lay behind him, where he knew there would be safe houses. Then he saw the IRA fighters to his left abandon the woods and start up the hill toward him. He stepped forward.

"Face left," he yelled. "Cover your mates making for the pass."

Rifle barrels swung to the left in unison and poured fire down on the police. Most of the Newport men made it to safety behind the IRA lines. The wounded tried to follow. A few were surrounded, marched back down the hill, and loaded into the lorries. Many bodies lay motionless on the grass.

As the police advanced, the Newport fighters reached the ridge and joined the defensive line. Bud saw Michael Kilroy and Joe Ring heading for the pass, Joe's brothers Walter and Jack covering their rear. "We have to get the wounded out of here," he shouted.

"How do we do that?" Kilroy yelled.

"Post snipers above the pass," Bud called. "Keep the police from following too close as we withdraw."

Joe Ring shouted to his brothers, and they fanned out to the other columns, ordering riflemen up the mountain pass sides.

"Get the wounded into the pass," Bud yelled. A bleeding Joe Gill staggered toward them, and he left the line to slide an arm around his shoulders. The rest of the IRA refugees thronged through the pass, the last group, commanded by Walter and Jack Ring, covering their withdrawal. Gill groaned, and Bud let him down to the ground.

"Joe! Joe, are you all right?"

No answer. Bud spied Kevin working his way back into the pass. "Kevin! Help me!"

Kevin dropped his rifle, and together they hooked their arms around Joe's shoulders and dragged him toward the pass. When he groaned, they hesitated. "Come on, Joe," Bud muttered. "We have to keep moving."

Together, they dragged the wounded man another 50

feet, but suddenly Bud realized Joe was no longer breathing. They let him slip to the ground, and Bud checked for a pulse. Nothing.

"Kevin, we have to leave him. We can come back for him later."

The IRA sniper fire covering their retreat began to slack off, but bodies littered the pass. Bud and Kevin caught up with the rest of the fighters and finally reached the exit to the pass where he could see the hamlet of Skerdagh below him. There were perhaps 20 frame houses and smaller thatched cottages scattered around a post office, a small church, and a burned-out police barracks.

The shooting behind them stopped. *Thank God they're not going to chase us through the pass.*

The men stumbled into the town, where Joe Ring and Michael Kilroy directed them to safe houses. "Meet at the church before dawn," Joe called. "The constables and Tans will probably come first thing in the morning; I want us all out of here before then."

Before Kilroy and the Ring brothers did a head count, Bud checked the pass. It was empty and quiet.

"How many did we lose?" Kilroy asked.

"Nine are missing," Joe said heavily. "Six more are wounded."

"We'll hide here overnight," Kilroy said. "Stay on the

lookout for stragglers."

Joe assigned Bud and Kevin to the Mungovan house. Just as the sun was sinking below the horizon, they knocked on the door.

An older man opened to them. "IRA," Bud intoned. The door swung wide.

"Welcome," the gray-haired man said. "You two look like you had a pretty rough time. Go on out back and clean up a bit while my wife fixes you somethin' to eat."

In Mungovan's backyard, Kevin and Bud washed up at the pump and shook the dirt from their clothes. Bud constantly checked the pass above them for Tans and constables, and then he noticed that blood spattered his jacket and trousers. Maybe Joe Gill's.

When they returned to the house, Mr. Mungovan pressed a glass of something cloudy into Bud's hands. "It's my homemade poteen," the old man said. "Mind yourself, it's a mite strong."

Bud downed it in one swallow. "Ah, God love ya, Mr. Mungovan, 'tis the drink of kings."

"Call me Ed," the older man said with a smile.

Kevin sipped his. "We'd best keep our wits about us," he cautioned.

"So," Ed Mungovan said, lowering his voice, "what happened up there in the mountains?"

For a moment Bud just stared into his glass, unable to speak. "What happened?" he said at last. "We were shot up pretty bad. No thanks to the Westport boys."

Mungovan nodded as his elderly wife in a faded housedress brought in a platter of boiled potatoes along with some cheese, a loaf of bread, and a plate of thinly sliced ham. "We don't have much," she said. "But you're welcome to it."

"You're risking your lives takin' us in," Kevin said. "It's not likely we'll be findin' fault with the supper."

After they ate their fill, Bud and Kevin bedded down on the parlor floor. Bud slept badly. *I don't want the Tans to find us here. It would go badly for this kindly old couple.* After another sleepless hour he threw off the wool blanket and quietly slipped out the back door.

"Bud?" Joe Ring's voice stopped him in his tracks. "What are you doing out?"

"Couldn't sleep. Guess I'm waitin' for the Tans to show up."

Ring pushed some dirt around with the toe of his boot. "You think they're really going to come here?"

"They can read a map, can't they?"

Joe nodded, and after a long moment Bud went back inside the house.

Before dawn he heard the growl of trucks coming toward Skerdagh. He jabbed Kevin's shoulder, and the two tiptoed through the house and into the street.

Michael Kilroy's tense voice suddenly boomed out of the dark. "Take cover," he ordered. They and the other men who had gathered by the church slipped behind houses and trees just as two Chesley lorries and a squad car braked to a stop. Bud pulled his Bulldog out of his trouser pocket and took aim.

The first shot came from his left, and suddenly all hell broke loose.

Chapter Seventeen

A Message

Squads of constables and Tans moved in, and the IRA fighters scattered in every direction.

"Kevin," Bud whispered from behind a tree. "There's too many of them, and they're way too good. We have to get out of here." His brother nodded, and they worked their way back behind the houses, keeping out of sight of the police. They picked their way over the foothills, then through fields and pastures, staying away from the roads. As they put the miles between themselves and Skerdagh, the pop and whine of gunfire grew fainter and more sporadic.

They headed south toward Westport, deciding to skirt the town of Kilmeena, and by the time the sun was directly overhead, they were well past it. By suppertime they had reached the outskirts of Westport, and they picked up a well-worn path through a field to avoid the main street. They skirted the tavern and came in the back door.

Mike was behind the bar. When he saw them, he finished serving the customers and met them in the kitchen with a relieved look. "I'm glad to see you two," he exclaimed. "Where have you been? Rose and Maggie are goin' crazy downstairs. They wanted to go out and hunt for you!"

"No need, Mike. It was a mess, but we're here now, and we're hungry." Bud made two tomato and cheese sandwiches and had just taken his first bite when Mike reappeared with a copy of the Mayo Times and dropped it on the counter. The headline caught Bud's attention. "Maggie Ludden Sought for Questioning in Blackharbor Murders."

Bud put his sandwich down. "What's this?"

"Two of the Tans who survived at Blackharbor recognized her. The constables came here earlier lookin' to arrest her for murder."

"Arrest Maggie? Why *her*? There were a good dozen of us at Blackharbor."

"They recognized her, that's why," Mike said. "She's in the cellar with Rose, worried that you were dead. And," he continued after a long pause, "we haven't heard anything from Walter."

"By all the saints ..." Bud grabbed his sandwich, pounded down the basement stairs, and rapped twice on the cellar wall. "Rose? It's Bud."

She slid the panel open and launched herself at him. Holding his sandwich out of the way, he wrapped his free arm around her and kissed her cheek.

"Where have you been?" she cried. "The newspaper said the police killed some IRA fighters and captured some that were injured. Maggie and I thought you were dead or wounded or sittin' in prison somewhere."

"Not dead," Bud muttered. "Just bloody tired."

Maggie appeared. "Did you see Walter? Why isn't he with you?"

"I saw him yesterday mornin' before dawn. After that it was thick fightin', and ..."

Maggie turned white. "Oh, dear God."

"This mornin' was the last time we saw anyone before the police launched their second ambush at Skerdagh. Kevin and I got away just in time."

Mike appeared on the stairs. "Bud, there's somethin' else you should know. The English have dumped our dead and wounded from Kilmeena in front of the constables' office. Just dumped them in the street."

Bud gritted his teeth. "They're sendin' the IRA a

message. They have no respect for us."

"We were goin' to take in some of the wounded," Rose said. "But the constables were watchin' and takin' down the names of people tryin' to help."

Maggie touched his arm. "We recruited some sympathizers from out of town to come and help, but ..." She swallowed. "That took time. We don't know how many died right there in front of the constables' office."

Bud swore. "Bloody bastards."

"They gave no care to the wounded," Rose added. "The sympathizers from Claremorris and Foxford came to town and led some of the wounded away. They came in cars and trucks, but they had to scatter before the police arrested them. Maggie and I went out in the street with a lot of the townspeople to cause as much interference as we could so our friends could get to the wounded."

"What about the dead?" Bud asked in a quiet voice.

"The coroner came for them. Bud, everybody in town is outraged. Everyone in the county had a friend or a relative just dumped in the street! The Mayo Times even interviewed the Marquess of Sligo, and in the newspaper, she severely criticized the English."

Bud blew out his cheeks. "Mike, you'd better get back upstairs and tend bar. Kevin and I are goin' to change clothes and eat something more."

He then tried to explain to Rose and Maggie how the Kilmeena operation had gone wrong. "The Westport column is one reason. They just didn't show up!"

He tramped upstairs to his room, changed his blood-stained clothes, and headed back down to the bar where Rose waited. Just as he arrived, the back door banged open, and Jack and Walter Ring came in. Jack's arm was in a sling.

Bud started toward them. "Jack, what happened to you?"

"I got clipped in the pass during the escape to Skerdagh. 'Tis only a flesh wound, no bones broken, but it hurts like the devil."

"Walter," Rose said quietly, "Maggie's worried sick about you. You'd better let her know you're all right." Without a word, Walter headed down to the cellar.

Bud tipped his head toward the sandwich he still held in his hand. "Jack, would you be hungry?"

"Ravenous."

"Then sit yourself down at that back table and I'll fix you somethin' to eat. Mike will bring you a pint."

After a few minutes Walter rejoined them, and Bud set the teakettle on the stove and sliced bread for sandwiches. In a few minutes he slid a plate of food in front of Jack and Walter and sat down at the table with them. "What are we goin' to do now?" he asked.

Jack sent him a sharp look. "We're gettin' together out at Claddy tomorrow. Can you make it out there?"

Bud leaned back in his chair. *Jesus, can't we even bury our dead before starting up again?*

"I know what you're thinkin'," Jack said.

"And how would you know that?"

"Look, it's only a meetin' to talk about what we do next. I'd like you and Kevin to come and lend your opinions."

Bud drew in a slow breath but said nothing until Jack leaned forward. "I'm hopin' you'll come. I'll send a car around to pick you up."

"All right," Bud said at last. *Lord, I hope I'm doing the right thing. For both Rose and myself.*

* * *

The next morning, Bud and Kevin arrived at Leenaun Road near Claddy, along with other vehicles, carriages, horses, and men on foot. The minute they arrived, Joe Ring took them aside. "Michael Kilroy just got word that the Tans passed by here on their way to Carrowkennedy. Beyond Carrowkennedy is the Erriff Bridge, and yesterday Kilroy sent some of our men to destroy that bridge. When the Tans come back this way, we'll be waitin' for them."

Bud scanned the gathering and counted at least 45 men

gathered in Jim McDole's farmyard at Claddy; then he looked up the road toward the Erriff Bridge. "When do you think they'll be comin' back this way?"

Joe looked up the road and shrugged. "I'm guessin' another thirty minutes."

Bud gestured at the crowd. "Where did all these people come from?"

"Brodie Malone's boys are here from Westport," Joe explained. "I really let him have it about Kilmeena. Brodie apologized and made excuses, and I told him I wasn't interested in his excuses. The Newport column got here an hour ago, and the Louisburgh Volunteers are here as well. You're assigned to fight under Malone's command. Carrowkennedy is a few hundred yards up the road, so right now we need to get in place."

"Get into place? I thought this was a meetin', not a fight."

"We tried to get word to you earlier. We intended it to be a meetin' until we got word that the Tans were passin' right by here. The other columns brought their firearms and ammunition. Bud, pick out a rifle for yourself; we're going to need you."

Michael Kilroy yelled, "Let's go, lads! We need to get everybody in place."

Bud moved out with the rest of the men. "Joe, do you

have a plan?"

"You'll hear it from Michael Kilroy when we get there."

At the bridge, Michael Kilroy held up his hand and waited until everyone arrived and had gathered around him. "I want the Westport lads to take positions behind that stone wall over there. Remove some of the stones to make firing loopholes. The Newport men will position themselves farther west, in the woods that extend from the stone wall." He paused and drew in a long breath.

"The Louisburgh Volunteers will be on the other side of the road, up on that ridge over there." He pointed behind him. "They'll have the best view of the junction with the road to Drummin."

Bud studied the stone wall Kilroy had indicated. *Not a bad spot. Lots of cover.*

"We learned some lessons at Kilmeena," Kilroy continued. "This time we're goin' to hold our fire until all the vehicles, both Chesley lorries and the police car, are within firing range. The lorry in the lead will draw fire, then the other lorry and the Ford can't surprise us. Expect the lead lorry to be some distance ahead of the other Chesley and the squad car. This time we wait until all three vehicles are within firing range, then we open up all at once. Is that clear?"

He nodded as the crowd murmured approval, then

continued. "I have assigned six snipers in three groups. Each pair of snipers will target a different vehicle and shoot to kill the driver. That way the Tans won't have a chance to form a protective barricade like they did at Kilmeena. Once all the vehicles have stopped, they'll unload their Lewis machine gun."

"Lewis machine gun?" someone called. "They had a Jennings at Kilmeena."

"Guess they wanted more flexibility," Kilroy answered. "So, they went for a Lewis instead of the Jennings. At any rate, the primary target for the snipers and the boys on the wall is the machine gun crew. We have to take out their heavy gun early."

At that moment a young blond boy ran up to Kilroy and whispered something in his ear. "Thanks, Sean," Kilroy muttered. "Good lad." The boy then headed back up the road in the direction of Erriff Bridge.

Kilroy propped his hands on his hips. "The Tans have reached Erriff Bridge and have stopped at Darby Hasting's pub. I'm guessin' they'll probably put away a lot of ale." He surveyed the crowd and smiled. "That's good for us. I would like nothin' better than to kill a lot of drunken Tans. I figure they'll be comin' through here around six-thirty. Young Sean will warn us when they're getting' back in their lorries."

He paused. "Any questions?"

Bud had a few, but he held his tongue. *No point in poking at a good plan.*

Kilroy waited a full minute. "All right, men, take your positions." Then he grinned.

Bud climbed over the stone wall and removed a few loose stones to make his firing loop, then retrieved a Lee-Enfield rifle from Brodie Moran and sighted up and down the road for practice. It would be another hour before the firing started, so he climbed on top of the stone wall and tried to relax.

Some of the men lit pipes or cigarettes. Others made small talk to fill the time while the sun passed overhead. Finally, Bud spied young Sean trotting toward them.

"They're on their way," the boy shouted.

The men scrambled into position. Bud looked over the wall and was amazed at how well they were hidden. Then someone yelled, "Here they come!" and he heard the whine of a truck engine coming from the direction of Erriff Bridge.

The men stamped out their cigarettes and waited.

Chapter Eighteen

Carrowkennedy

When the first lorry approached on the road leading between the Westport men stationed behind the stone wall and the Louisburgh Volunteers on the ridge, the IRA riflemen opened fire. Instantly the Chesley sped up, but snipers sighted on the driver and shot him. The lorry then veered off the road into a grassy field where it coasted to a stop. The Tan driver inside was slumped across the steering wheel.

The tailgate then banged open, and Black and Tans jumped out and began unloading the pieces of a Lewis machine gun. While the gun crew assembled it, a protective cordon of Tans surrounded it.

The IRA men kept firing. Finally, the cordon of Tans stepped away, and the man operating the machine gun swung the barrel up toward the ridge and fired two short bursts. Almost instantly the gunner was shot dead. Another Tan then jumped behind the gun, took aim, and fired a single burst. He, too, was hit and slumped forward. A third Tan pulled the body away, but before he could swing the gun barrel toward the bridge, he was shot as well.

The second Chesley arrived. Two sniper bullets penetrated the windshield, and the truck crashed into the shallow ditch parallel to the road. Its tailgate clanked open, and a swarm of Tans poured out to form a defensive circle with the lorry at their backs. One of the Tans attached a grenade launcher to his rifle, then launched the missile at the stone wall where Bud lay hidden. The men ducked down, but the grenade fell short and the shrapnel bounced harmlessly off the stone wall. None of the men were hurt.

The rebel fire intensified, and still the Tans kept shooting. Then they launched another grenade, this time in the direction of the Louisburgh Volunteers lines. It sailed over their heads and exploded harmlessly on the far side of the ridge.

The squad car arrived and passed the crippled lorries. IRA snipers took out the driver, and the vehicle careened off the road, crossed into a grassy field, and smacked into a small cottage. The escaping Tans broke down the cottage door and took cover inside.

Behind the stone wall, Brodie Malone shouted that the Tans were out of ammunition and were loading a new drum on the Lewis. He stood up, yelling, "Charge the machine gun." Bud and the rest of the Westport men scrambled over the wall and ran toward the stricken Chesley. The surviving Tans saw them coming, retreated behind the second lorry, and escaped into the cottage.

The men of the Westport column lay on their bellies and spread out in front of the cottage. Then Michael Kilroy ordered another group around the back to surround it, and Bud gritted his teeth. *Looks like we've got a siege.*

The standoff lasted for hours. Finally, when the sun set and darkness crept over the area, Bud watched a three-quarter moon rise, illuminating wispy clouds overhead. The entire landscape looked eerie.

Four IRA men jockeyed their Lewis machine gun into position in front of the cottage and loaded a fresh drum of bullets. One of the men flopped down behind the gun, gripped the handle, and put his index finger on the trigger, ready to fire.

Suddenly Joe Ring stood over the crew. "Stand down," he said quietly.

The trigger man looked up. "What?"

"I said stand down. That's the Widow O'Connor's cottage. Her husband died in an IRA shootout with the Tans a year ago. Since then she's many times allowed us to use her home as a safe house, so we're not goin' to shoot up that cottage until we know she and her son are safe."

For half an hour everything was quiet. Moonlight bathed the countryside, and a faint light flickered through the front cottage window. Apparently, the Tans inside had lit candles.

They waited in tense silence. All at once the front door banged open, and a middle-aged woman with grey hair wearing an apron was pushed outside. The door slammed behind her.

She took two steps away from the cottage and stopped facing Michael Kilroy. "Mrs. O'Connor," he yelled. "What do you want?"

"The Tans want me to bring them more ammunition," she called. "I told them I would not. But they have my son David inside. They said if I didn't get the ammunition, they would hurt him." She folded her arms across her chest. "I will not do it."

Kilroy walked toward the cottage. "Hello the house!" he shouted. "Who's in charge?"

A big man with a blond handlebar mustache opened the front door. "That would be me. Sergeant-Major Wilson."

"If anythin' happens to the Widow O'Connor or her son, we will kill every last Tan inside. Do you understand?"

"I hear ya." After a long pause, the soldier added, "What are you proposing?"

"Send out young O'Connor. Then give up your weapons and we'll let you live."

The sergeant-major paused in the doorway, then stepped back inside the house. After a tense few minutes, the door opened again and a young boy stumbled out. The lad scampered to his mother, and they stood locked in an embrace.

"Mrs. O'Connor," Ring called. "Come on over here."

The woman and the boy moved behind the Republican firing line, and then the cottage door flew open once more and a collection of rifles and revolvers were tossed out on the ground. Finally, Sergeant-Major Wilson reappeared. "That's the lot," he shouted.

"Wait there a minute," Ring called. He motioned to Kilroy, then turned to Bud. "Ryan, grab a few men. There are spare petrol cans on the Chesley. Get all the firearms and ammunition out of the lorries, then set fire to them. When we get the Tans out of the cottage, we'll pull the squad car away from the house and burn it, too."

"Colin, Pat, Mickey, Sean," Bud called. "Come with me." They pulled the petrol can off the first Chesley, soaked the lorry with gasoline, and lit it. Then they moved to the other vehicle and repeated the process. While the two Chesleys burned, Kilroy ordered the Tans out of the cottage.

Sixteen Tans filed out with their hands in the air. Kilroy ordered them to stand away from the house while Bud's crew pulled the squad car 30 feet away, doused it, and set it on fire. Once it was engulfed in flames, Kilroy gestured to the sergeant-major and pointed back down the road toward Westport.

"You're free to go."

The sergeant-major spat at him, then turned to his men. "Let's go, boys. We have a long trek ahead of us."

Kilroy turned to find Joe Ring beside him. "How did we do?"

"The Tans have eight dead," Joe replied. "We lost no one, but a couple of our lads have minor wounds."

"What about their weapons?" Kilroy asked.

Ring turned to Bud. "Do you have an inventory?"

"We captured twenty-two rifles, eight drums for the Lewis machine gun, several boxes of grenades, twenty-one revolvers, and about six thousand rounds of rifle ammunition."

Ring nodded, and he and Michael Kilroy surveyed the blazing Chesleys. "The Tans won't be happy about this," Kilroy muttered after a moment. "We should expect reprisals, so anybody here that's known to them should go on the run. Joe Ring has a list of safe houses where you can hide, but everyone else should watch himself." He paused and looked at the flickering flames. "Well done, men. This is a great victory for Ireland."

* * *

As soon as he got back to the tavern, Bud went down to the cellar. "Rose." He touched her shoulder. "Rose, wake up. I want to tell you what happened."

She rolled over and sat up. "Bud! Where have you been? I thought you just went to a meetin'. What time is it?"

Maggie stirred. "What's goin' on?" she said, her voice drowsy.

Bud pulled Rose close, then kissed her. "It wasn't a meetin', Rose. By the time I got to Claddy, Michael Kilroy announced that the Tans were about to drive right through Carrowkennedy. He'd already contacted three IRA columns from around Westport, so we had forty or fifty fighters there. We killed eight of them."

Maggie sat up and leaned toward Bud. "Was Walter there?"

"He was."

She sucked in her breath. "Is he all right?"

"More than all right."

She sank back onto her pillow. "Thank God," she murmured.

Rose wound her arms around him. "Bud, listen to me. I want you to stop goin' out with the IRA men. We have plans for our future, and they don't include you gettin' hurt or killed."

Bud squeezed her shoulder. "Rose, we're close to winnin'. Carrowkennedy was a huge success." He went on to describe the details of the interrupted meeting and the attack. Finally, he glanced over at Maggie. "You don't seem pleased, Maggie."

"Oh, well I am, to be sure. But ..." she hesitated. "Rose, tell him about that new directive from London."

Bud stopped breathing. "What new directive?"

"The directive to burn IRA sympathizers' homes as official reprisal has been rescinded," Maggie said. "The Tans and constables are not allowed to do that anymore."

"That's good news, if I understand it correctly. We're makin' progress."

"Now," Rose said, her voice flat. "Give him the bad news."

Bud's heart stopped. "Bad news?"

Rose looked at him. "England has made the partition of Northern Ireland from Ireland permanent. King George traveled to Belfast and has attended the swearin' in of a prime minister for Northern Ireland."

Bud almost choked. "A lot of people won't be happy about that."

"But," she added, "it's also a back-handed acknowledgment of the Irish Republic. Maybe this could end all the bloodshed."

He nodded. "We're goin' to celebrate tomorrow evening. Maybe Kevin can get the Shamrocks to play at the pub."

Rose looked over at her sister. "Mike told us there's a thousand-pound bounty on Maggie. I think we should stay down here in the cellar."

"Ah, no, Rose. You two have been cooped up here for too long. Besides, no constables or Protestants are allowed in Ryan Brothers tavern."

Rose hugged him. "I'll sing you a ballad, Bud." She hugged him again and pulled the quilt up around her shoulders. Maggie just looked at him.

The next night when Bud arrived at the bar, Kevin and Mike were already preparing for a busy night. Customers had begun to arrive late that afternoon, and by six the Shamrocks had arrived. Red-haired fiddle player Seamus Conway stepped forward, his instrument in his hand.

"Good evening, lads and lasses. We'd like to offer a tune called 'A Nation Once Again'. Sing along with us if ye'd like."

He nodded to the drummer, and the three-member group raised their voices.

"When boyhood's fire was in my blood,

I read of ancient freemen

For Greece and Rome who bravely stood,

Three hundred men and three men.

And then I prayed I yet might see,

Our fetters rent in twain,

And Ireland, long a province, be ...

A Nation once again."

By the second chorus, the tavern was jam-packed and everyone was joining in. Bud went down to the cellar to get Rose and Maggie, and by the time they entered the bar, Jack and Walter Ring had arrived. Before Seamus and the band began playing again, the fiddle player invited the audience to request a number.

"Do you know 'The Irish Rover'?" Rose called out.

"Oh, aye, lass, so we do."

"If you'll play that tune, my sister and I will dance."

A murmur ran through the crowd. The music started up, and Rose and Maggie stepped into the center of the room and began to dance, their upper bodies stiff, their kicks precise. As the tempo increased, people began to clap in time to the music. He'd seen Rose dance before, at church socials, but this was different. She wasn't smiling, and her eyes looked wet.

Bud was standing behind the bar when he noticed two men furtively slip out the front door. Instantly he slapped down his polishing rag and went to find Walter.

"Get Maggie out of here," he hissed.

Walter frowned. "Why? She's enjoyin' herself for a change."

"A couple of men at the bar took one look at the girls and left all of a sudden. For that matter, you'd better get Rose out of here, too. They'd love to get their hands on her."

"Jesus," Walter breathed. "And there's still that bounty on Maggie." He shouldered his way to the front of the crowd, and when the song ended, he approached the Ludden sisters. "Don't look around," he murmured, "but we need to get you out of the tavern."

Maggie blinked at him. "But ..."

"*Now*, Maggie. Rose, you need to come, too. I'll explain later."

Chapter Nineteen

Escape and Trouble

Walter and Jack Ring elbowed their way back through the crowd and headed for the back door with Maggie and Rose in tow. Bud trailed after them. "Where are you taking them?"

"We'll let you know," Jack said over his shoulder, then followed Walter and the girls outside.

The band had just launched into another song when a uniformed Constable Harris and another constable marched in the front door. Before they'd gone more than three steps, Mike stepped into their path. "Constable Harris, you know you're not welcome in this tavern." As he spoke, another pair of constables burst in through the back door.

"We're here on official business, Ryan," Constable Harris growled. He stretched up and surveyed the crowd. "Maggie Ludden was seen in here."

"Nah," Mike drawled. "Somebody's been tellin' you a tall story. Maggie Ludden is not here."

"I don't believe you," Harris snapped. He marched over to the band and halted their music. Angry shouts erupted from the crowd. Then, while his partner stood by the door, he turned toward the crowd and began to address them. "Now, you all know me—"

"Take your friends and get out!" a voice called from the back.

"Hold on a minute," Harris said. "We're not here to make trouble for you. We're here to arrest Maggie Ludden."

A number of men surged to their feet and shook their fists at the constable. "Get out of here, you damned English," one yelled. "You think we'd let you touch any of our women?"

The shouting from the crowd grew louder, and Bud stepped up to Constable Harris. "You'd better get out of here," he murmured. "Otherwise, you're goin' to have a riot on your hands for sure."

By now everyone in the pub was on their feet, yelling and punching their fists in the air. Harris continued to scan the crowd, but Bud shoved him toward the door. "Seamus," he shouted over his shoulder, "play a jig. Loud!"

The Shamrocks struck up a fast, Irish tune, and Mike and Kevin escorted the police off the premises. As the music blazed away, little by little the patrons resumed their seats, and the celebratory atmosphere returned. Bud stepped behind the bar and filled beer and shot glasses as fast as he could, but with every passing minute he couldn't help wondering where the Ring brothers were taking Rose and Maggie.

After two more fast tunes, Seamus convinced John McAnley to step up and sing "Erinn Go Bragh." By the time he concluded his solo, the crowd had settled down, and by early morning the last customer had left and the tavern was quiet. Bud and his brothers cleaned up the bar, then went up to bed.

He lay awake for hours, worrying about Maggie and Rose. The most obvious place the Ring brothers would take them was out to their farm. And, he reflected, the most foolish thing he could do was to go in search of them because Constable Harris most likely had men watching him. But he thought about it anyway.

He worried about his brothers, as well. His recent conversations with Mike and Kevin had been unsettling. Mike wanted to plan a demonstration in front of the constables' headquarters, and Kevin had started writing angry letters to the Mayo Times.

The next morning all he could think about was Rose and her safety, so he decided to go out to the Ring farm to see whether she was there with Maggie and whether she and her sister were all right. But first he went out to get the morning paper, then sat down with Mike and Kevin and unfolded it. The headline caught his attention because it was in extra-large type: "Truce Signed in Dublin."

Bud shot to his feet. "Hey, look at this!" His brothers leaned over the table, but neither one said much until Bud turned to page two. Mike peered over his shoulder to read the article aloud. "It says here Michael Collins and Arthur Griffith signed a truce with the British," he breathed. "So where was de Valera?"

"He must have given Collins and Griffith authority to negotiate the terms," Kevin said flatly.

Bud smoothed the page out. "That's odd, though, isn't it? I didn't think de Valera was the type to give up the spotlight. Anyway, let's see what the terms are."

"There's a cease fire," Mike read slowly. "Ireland stays partitioned, and we're to be an English dominion for a year before we gain independence."

Kevin slammed his hand down on the newspaper. "That's not a truce!" he exclaimed. "That's a bloody surrender. I can't believe de Valera agreed to this."

Bud rubbed his chin. "It kind of makes sense, though."

Mike jumped up and started to pace around the table. "How does that make sense, Bud? This plan won't work as long as Protestants are on Irish soil. We fought for six years, and now we're just going to lie down and take it? No! It won't work."

Kevin nodded. "I think this means immediate war. Terrible war."

"But we've got our Republic," Bud countered. "We have to wait a year, but then we'll be free from England. We've waited eight hundred years, so what's one more?"

His brothers shook their heads. "It's not acceptable," Kevin said, his voice quiet.

"Oh Jesus, we can't go on killin' and dyin' now, can we?" Bud stood up suddenly. "I'm goin' out to see Joe Ring. I've got to find out for sure where Rose and Maggie are."

He walked down to Keough's to borrow a horse, then headed out into the countryside, taking a circuitous route and checking constantly to make sure he wasn't followed. As he drew near the Ring farm, he noticed lookouts stationed on the hills. One of the sentries recognized him and waved him through.

He dismounted and walked up to the farmhouse, but before he could knock, Rose opened the door and threw her arms around him. "Oh, Bud, I knew you'd come!"

"Are you all right?"

"I am, for now. I know we can't stay here forever, but we didn't know where else to go."

Maggie stepped out from behind her sister and gave him a polite embrace, watched by Walter and Jack Ring who were sitting at the kitchen table with their arms folded across their chests. Bud held up his hands and declared, "Don't worry, lads. I made sure I wasn't followed."

"We saw the constables come into the tavern when we went out the back door," Rose said. "What did they want?"

"They were lookin' for Maggie. Jack and Walter got you out just in time."

Bud sat down at the kitchen table. "Where's your brother, Joe?" he asked.

"A runner came a few hours back," Walter answered. "Someone asked him to come to Paddy Burke's for a meetin'."

"A meetin'? Who with?"

"Michael Collins and the rest of the column commanders. It seems Collins and Arthur Griffith signed a truce, but nobody knows what's goin' on."

"They'd been in negotiations for months," Bud said. "Then all of a sudden they sign a truce? Doesn't make sense."

"Maybe it will soon," Jack offered. "That's why Joe went off to Paddy's. Michael Collins will be there, and he's supposed to explain everything."

All at once a faint voice from outside called, "Rider comin'." In the next moment Joe Ring exploded into the farmhouse.

"Bud? What are you doing here?"

"I came lookin' for Rose and Maggie. What happened in the meetin' at Burke's?"

"Michael Collins read a proclamation from Eamon de Valera. I've a copy right here." He slipped a paper out of his pocket and laid it on the table.

Bud bent over it. "Proclamation," he read aloud. "Fellow citizens, during this period of truce each individual soldier and citizen must regard himself as a custodian of the nation's honor. Your discipline must prove in the most convincing manner that this is the struggle of an independent nation."

He stopped until Rose jiggled his arm, and he went on. "In the negotiations now initiated, your representatives will do their utmost to acquire a just and peaceful termination of this struggle."

"A bit wordy, don't you think?" Joe Ring grumbled. "Sounds ... I don't know, too formal."

"Maybe," Bud said.

Joe continued reading. "History, particularly our own history, and the character of the issue to be decided warn us against undue confidence."

"Oh, Lord save us," Rose murmured. "Are we not to believe in this truce?"

Bud put his hand over hers and squeezed it. Joe continued reading. "An unbending determination to endure all that may be necessary, and the fortitude you have shown in your recent sufferings alone will lead you to the peace you desire."

"Jesus," Jack Ring muttered.

"There's more," Joe said. "Should force be resumed against our nation we must once more be ready to resist. Thus, you will secure the final abandonment of force and the acceptance of justice and reason as the arbiter." He heaved a sigh. "It's signed by Eamon de Valera."

No one said a word. Finally, Bud looked over at Joe. "What do you think?"

"The commanders of all the Mayo columns pledged support for the cease fire and for the treaty," Joe answered. "We stand with de Valera."

"Do you think everyone will honor this cease fire?"

Joe closed his eyes. "I don't know. But they'd better."

"What about the bounty on our Maggie?" Rose asked.

"Maggie's wanted for actin' against the English at Blackharbor," Joe said heavily. "And we're still a dominion of England. I don't think Maggie will be safe until the

Republic is free. So, for now she needs to stay hidden."

Maggie turned away and began to cry.

"But," Joe continued. "We've done it. The English will be leavin', and for that we should celebrate."

Walter stepped forward and folded Maggie into his arms, while Bud held Rose close for a long minute without speaking. Joe went to the cupboard and took out a bottle of Irish whiskey, set out six shot glasses, and filled them. "Erinn go bragh," he said solemnly. All six raised their glasses. "Erinn go bragh."

He poured them full again. "At some point the Republic will have to form an army, and de Valera has appointed me Officer in Charge of the IRA in Westport. They're thinkin' that I might contribute to this new army, but in the meantime I'm the liaison for County Galway to coordinate our efforts and bring organization to western Ireland. I'll be leavin' this afternoon for Galway to meet with the new government officials."

"Why Galway?" Bud asked. "It's so far away. Why not County Sligo or someplace closer to Westport?"

"Seems I've got somethin' of a reputation in County Galway," Joe said slowly. "Because I'm really an outsider there, I'm eligible to mediate conflicts."

"Sounds like a big job," Bud remarked. "And maybe thankless as well."

"Maybe. I have to get a handle on our own County Mayo people. Turnin' from waging guerilla warfare to functioning as an independent country is goin' to take time."

Bud had heard enough. He decided to take Rose for a walk so they could be private and talk. When they'd tramped out of earshot from the house, he turned to her. "I can tell somethin' is botherin' you, Rose. What is it?"

Rose studied the grass beneath their feet. "Maggie told me Walter wants to leave Ireland and take her to America. They want to know if I'll go with them."

"But you're engaged to me," he protested.

"I know."

Bud studied her tense face. "Are you thinkin' about goin' to America? Does that mean you want to break off our engagement?"

"No, Bud, of course not. But maybe we should think about gettin' away from here. Would we do better in America?"

Bud pulled her into his arms and kissed her. "Maggie and Walter have to consider goin' to America. There's a bounty on Maggie's head, and in America she'd be safe."

"But ... but Maggie's my sister. Now she's my only livin' relative, and I'd miss her so much I—" Her voice broke.

"Is Walter really goin' to do this? Go off to America?"

She tried to smile. "Right now, they're just talkin'.

They've made no final plans."

"What about you, Rose? What do you want?"

"Oh, Bud," she sighed. "Right now, I want to stay here. My future is with you, here in Ireland. But I know that eventually we'll have to decide about our life here in Ireland."

He slid his arm around her waist and pulled her close. "I don't want Maggie to leave either, Rose. But she and Walter have to do what's best for them."

* * *

Back at the tavern that afternoon, Bud spoke briefly to his brothers about de Valera's proclamation. "We should have a big crowd tonight to celebrate the treaty. Kevin, maybe you could ask the Shamrocks to play again."

"Aye, I will. But ..."

"But? But what, Kev?"

"Paddy Burke stopped by to warn us that this truce could break down at any time. If the English renege and we're back at war, we should be ready to fight. And ..." He hesitated. "I'm not so sure this treaty is the right thing."

Mike swiped his bar rag across the counter. "Up in Sligo, the IRA, the constables, and the Tans are still settlin' old scores. People are still bein' murdered."

Bud just looked at him and slowly shook his head. "We have another whole year to live with the English. If people think they have to settle scores, this whole thing could come apart. I'm worried about this treaty, too. I don't think this is the final answer and I'm worried that things could get out of control."

The three brothers looked at each other in silence.

They opened the tavern at four that afternoon, and it quickly filled up. In another hour the Shamrocks were playing, and between tunes Bud talked with the customers about the treaty. Most were distrustful.

"We object to the partition of Northern Ireland," one man announced loudly. "We haven't really driven the bastards out of Ireland, now have we?"

Another customer, Mike Green, voiced his fears over a shot of whiskey. "The British could build up a proper army in Northern Ireland, re-invade, and take back all of Ireland."

Then Joe Walsh walked in and ordered a pint. Though he made the rounds shaking hands and voicing congratulations, Bud sensed an undercurrent of disbelief that the treaty would hold up. "The IRA," someone shouted, "is ready to go back to the fight!"

The Shamrocks finished up a little after midnight, but the bar stayed open until 2:30 in the morning. Bud decided the treaty and the de Valera proclamation were a step in the right direction, a step toward peace. He'd already seen too much violence, both in France and here in County Mayo; it was time to think about Rose and their future together.

I don't want to be working in a tavern for the rest of my life. I need a proper job so I can finally marry Rose. There's sure to be good jobs opening up after the treaty is put in place, maybe even a job in the new Irish army.

The next morning when Bud went downstairs, he found Kevin and Mike enjoying their breakfast of scrambled eggs and tea. Bud joined them and filled his plate, but he'd barely pulled up a chair when Kevin pointed his fork at him. "Where does Joe Ring stand with this treaty?"

"He's for it. Michael Collins appointed him commander of the IRA units in County Mayo."

"So, he's going to enforce the treaty?" Kevin pursued.

"That's what I'm told."

Kevin frowned. "Well, you stay away from Joe Ring. You hear me? Stay away from him. If this treaty falls apart, we don't want you on the wrong side."

"By the way," Mike asked, "Where are Rose and Maggie?"

"Out at the Ring farm. I'm headed out that way when I finish eatin'."

Kevin sent Mike a long look, then held Bud's gaze. "We want you to bring Rose and Maggie back here."

"What? Why? She and Maggie are safe enough out at the Ring farm."

Mike looked away, then focused on his empty plate. "Keep them away from Joe Ring and his brothers, Bud. They're trouble."

Chapter Twenty

Anarchy

The next morning Bud decided to bicycle out to the Ring farm. When he arrived, Jack and Walter were working in the barn, and he found Rose and Maggie in the farmhouse doing some housecleaning. He took Rose for a walk into an adjoining pasture, where they strolled to a spreading oak tree in the middle of the field and sat down to have a little privacy.

He took her into his arms and kissed her again and again. Then he took a deep breath and asked her about what had been preying on his mind. "What would you think about me volunteerin' for Joe Ring's new Irish Army?"

She went pale. "But why, Bud? I thought you didn't like all this violence."

"It would be a real job. If Joe takes me on, we could get married. I can't be tendin' bar with my brothers for the rest of my life, Rose. We need to start our own life."

"Well …," she hesitated. "Have you thought about bein' a constable? What that would mean?"

"Policin' isn't what I really want to do. It's not what I believe in, but I do believe in the treaty. And I have military experience. I could be useful. And if I joined the new army unit with Joe, we could get married and save enough money to buy our own place somewhere."

"That sounds almost too good to be true," she said softly.

He sighed. "There's another problem that's been on my mind, too. My brothers are against the treaty. They say we should keep fightin', and they think Joe Ring is wrong to defend the treaty. They want me to stay away from him. They say he's trouble."

She stared at him. "But Maggie and I live at the Rings' farm!"

"Yeah. That's a big problem."

"I want this treaty to hold so we can get on with our lives," she said. "But I can't go back to your cellar, Bud. I just can't. It's like a prison down there." She smoothed her hand over his shirt sleeve. "I'd better get back. Maggie and I were only halfway through the breakfast dishes."

They started for the house just as Joe Ring drove up in

a black car. They followed him inside, and while Rose joined Maggie in the kitchen, Bud took Joe aside. "Joe, when are you going to start puttin' together this new military unit? I'm thinkin' of joining."

"It's funny you should ask. I need to recruit an entire unit of County Mayo men, ones I can trust. Might you accept a commission as a captain? I want you to lead a company of volunteers."

Bud felt a rush of pride. "That's flatterin', Joe. Thanks."

Joe nodded. "I want my brother, Jack, to be my adjutant, and I've offered Walter a position as well. Talk it over with Rose, why don't you?"

"I thought Walter wanted to go to America with Maggie?"

"Not now. I need him here now. Maybe later."

"There's just one thing," Bud said hesitantly. "Where would this company be stationed?"

"The army I recruit will be keepin' the peace in Mayo and the surrounding counties. I plan to set up my headquarters in Westport."

Bud nodded.

"And I'm goin' to need a secretary. Rose?" he called into the kitchen. "Would you be interested in workin' for the new army?"

She appeared instantly. "Would I be paid?"

"Of course, you'd be paid. You could live here with Maggie until ... well, until you and Bud decide where you want to live."

"Maggie?" Rose called. "Did you hear?"

"I heard," Maggie called from the kitchen. Her voice sounded flat.

"Joe has asked Walter to join his new army," Bud put in.

Rose stiffened. "Maggie," she called to her sister. "I thought you and Walter were talkin' about going to America."

Maggie appeared, a dishtowel in one hand. "We were. Now Walter wants to see this treaty thing through, so he wants to stay in Ireland."

Bud left Rose and Maggie talking together in low tones, mounted his bicycle, and returned to the tavern just before they opened the bar. He cornered Kevin and Mike in the back storage room. "I've been offered a commission as captain in the new Irish army," he announced. "I'll be reporting to Joe Ring."

His brothers stared at him in silence. Then Kevin swore aloud. "I thought we told you to stay away from Joe Ring!"

"You did," Bud acknowledged. "But I want to help keep the peace under this treaty. And besides, Rose is stayin' out at the Rings' farm."

"This partition business stinks," Mike growled. "If I

were you, I'd wait to see which side your new army is going to take."

"Which side? *Which side?*" Bud repeated angrily. "Today we have a Republic. You want to keep the war goin'? Over what? Over Ulster? This new army is to maintain peace!"

He stormed away from his brothers and went down to the cellar to bring up more whiskey. They didn't speak again all evening, but working behind the bar, Bud listened to his customers talk. He was surprised to hear they were split on the treaty.

I can't believe some of them want more blood. Including my own brothers.

The next morning Bud again cycled out to the Ring farm to see Rose. Inside the farmhouse, he found Joe having a somber discussion with both his brothers and the Ludden sisters.

"What's going on?" Bud asked.

Joe turned to him. "What are you doing tomorrow, Bud? I want you to come with me to Galway. There's been some trouble."

"I'll have to see if I can take the time off, Joe."

Joe laughed. "You're done at the tavern, Captain Ryan. Your commission was approved this morning, and I'm needin' you tomorrow. I'll pick you up first thing in the mornin'.'"

Bud and Rose talked for a while out in the farmyard, then he headed back to the tavern. He wasn't sure how his brothers would react to his quitting, so he waited for a quiet moment before the bar opened.

"Kevin, Mike, I have somethin' to tell you."

Kevin folded his arms and eyed him skeptically. "What is it?"

He took a deep breath. "I'm quittin' the tavern to join Joe Ring's new army."

Mike squinted and closed one eye. "What did you say?"

"I said Joe Ring offered—"

"I heard that part," Mike shouted. "I mean about quittin' the tavern!"

"I said I'd have to quit to join—"

Mike threw his bar rag across the room. "What is the matter with you?" he shouted.

"So," Kevin growled, "you're willin' to sell out the Irish independence effort so you can play soldier?"

Bud straightened. "Now wait just one minute. I didn't 'play soldier' when I fought in France. I risked my goddamned life! Now we've earned the right to have an Irish Republic. Why can't you two get that through your heads?"

Kevin turned to Mike. "He's sellin' us out."

"I am not sellin' you out!" Bud shouted.

Kevin pointed to the back door. "Out," he ordered. "Get out. Get your things and get out."

"What?"

"I said get out!"

Bud's hands were shaking, so he balled his fists and swallowed the words that rose in his throat. *If this is the way it has to be, so be it. I have to do this. I have to.*

He turned away from them, climbed the stairs, and stuffed his clothes in his army duffel. Then he slipped his Bulldog into his jacket pocket. When he came back downstairs, he took a step toward his brothers, then thought better of it. *Their minds are made up. Well, so is mine.*

He went out and found his bicycle but couldn't manage it and his duffel, too, so he lugged it over to Keough's and borrowed a horse. When he arrived at the Ring farm, Rose met him at the door. She took one look at his face and gasped. "Bud! What's happened?"

"I told my brothers about my Irish army commission, and they threw me out."

The three Ring brothers gathered behind her. "Bad news, that," Walter said.

"Yeah. Look, would you mind if I slept here while I find a place to stay?"

"Sure," Joe said quickly. "We don't mind at all. Maybe you won't mind sleepin' in the barn for now."

"Thanks," Bud said.

"As a matter of fact," Joe continued, "I have to go down to Galway in the morning to look into some trouble. I want you to come with me."

Chapter Twenty-one

Galway

Bud made a nest in the barn loft, and when Rose was free, she climbed up and joined him. They stayed together until it was time for her and Maggie to start supper. Over the meal, Bud managed to ask Joe what was going on in Galway.

Joe put down his fork and leaned forward. "Some IRA fighters are roamin' around western Ireland murderin' former constables. As far as we can tell, these men didn't join any Republican units, so I figure they're tryin' to make a name for themselves after the fact. We call them 'Trucileers'. So, you and I are going down to Galway to investigate."

"Can't the constables take care of themselves?"

"The British disbanded the constables when they recalled the Tans, so now they no longer have the force of law or authority protectin' them. These Trucileers hunt the constables down and assassinate them. Three constables, Patrick Cassidy, Tobias Gibbons, and John Gilmartin, have been shot. They're in a hospital in Galway, and I need to find out what happened."

Bud said nothing, but he had lost his appetite.

The following morning, he and Joe drove off in Joe's Ford for the long trip to Galway. When they arrived at Galway Hospital, they went to the reception area and asked for Patrick Cassidy's room number. The antiseptic smell put Bud on edge; it reminded him of his months-long stay at the Dover rehabilitation hospital.

"Why are you here?" a well-muscled orderly inquired.

Joe introduced himself and Bud. "We're liaisons from Michael Collins and Eamon de Valera."

"Wait here while I get someone to talk to you." The orderly spun on his heel and moved away. Joe and Bud looked at each other, and a few minutes later a doctor in a white lab coat came toward them. "Are you Joe Ring?"

"I am."

"Come into my office, please." He led them to a small office where he turned to face them. "I'm Dr. McSorley, Chief of Staff here at Galway. I understand you're inquiring about Patrick Cassidy?"

"That's right."

Bud felt the hairs on the back of his neck start to itch.

"I'm sorry to tell you that Patrick Cassidy is dead," the doctor said, his voice quiet. "He was admitted two days ago with a gunshot wound in the back, but yesterday two men pushed their way into his room and shot him to death in his hospital bed."

"Jesus," Joe swore.

"The staff here is very upset," the doctor continued. "We had two officers from the new Irish police force here, but they didn't seem too experienced. Maybe you should talk to them."

In the next minute Joe was heading to the front entrance. "We need to get over to St. Bride's Hospital, that's where Tobias Gibbons and John Gilmartin are."

At the St. Bride's reception desk, Joe demanded to know which rooms Gibbons and Gilmartin occupied. The receptionist looked startled, then held up her hands. "I need to get my supervisor." A few minutes later she returned with a large woman in a business suit.

"And who might you be?" the woman inquired loudly.

Joe introduced himself, and the woman hesitated. "Unfortunately," she said at last, "we've had an incident. Last night two men stormed into the hospital rooms Mr.

Gibbons and Mr. Gilmartin occupied and shot them both."

Joe slammed his fist on the counter. "That's unconscionable! Bud, let's go talk to the police."

At the police station, Joe asked to speak to the officer investigating the murders of the three former constables. After an awkward silence, the desk sergeant escorted them to a small room with a battered desk and two visitor chairs. "Wait here."

After some minutes a young police officer with an officious manner stalked in and seated himself behind the desk. "Can I help you?"

"We're here to investigate the murders of three former constables," Joe said tightly. "Patrick Cassidy, Tobias Gibbons, and John Gilmartin."

The officer sent Joe a bland look. "We have requested no help from Dublin. We have the situation well under control."

Joe straightened and leaned over the man's desk. "I understand all three of these men were former constables, isn't that right?"

The young officer frowned. "I wasn't aware that these murders are connected. Yes, all three men were retired constables, but we're not sure why any of them were killed."

Joe stared at him for a long moment. "Let me understand this. Two gunmen go into two different hospitals and shoot three former constables in their beds and you don't see a connection?"

There was an awkward pause. Then the officer spoke again. "We're a little new at this," he ventured. "But we're getting help to understand what happened. When our investigation is complete, we will generate a report. If you leave your address, I will see to it that a copy is mailed to you."

Joe shot to his feet. "Never mind," he snapped. "Let's go, Bud." He didn't say another word until they climbed into Joe's car.

"We have to find Sean Garrity," Joe said, his face tense. "He's head of the IRA in Galway. Maybe he can tell us what happened here."

They stopped at a few businesses to make inquiries, and after a visit to a grocery, the proprietor told them Sean Garrity was usually at the Bull and Whistle Tavern at this time of day.

They pulled up at the Bull and Whistle and sat staring at the building. "Looks kind of rundown," Bud remarked. "Like it's seen its share of trouble. See those bullet holes just below the roof line?"

"I do," Joe said shortly.

"Joe, do you know this man, Garrity?"

"Only by reputation. He led the Volunteers down here in

Galway. There wasn't as much action here as there was in Mayo, but Sean Garrity's boys made their presence felt."

Bud nodded. "Is Garrity pro-treaty or anti-treaty? That could make a difference."

"I don't know where Garrity stands, and the same goes for his Volunteers. But they were loyal to the Republicans throughout our war with the Tans."

"Right."

"Bud," Joe asked suddenly. "Do you have your revolver?"

"I do. I carry it all the time now."

Joe shot him a look. "I have mine, too. We should stay alert."

Inside the small tavern, Bud couldn't help but notice the place looked pretty shabby with its dirt floor and the ancient thick stone walls. The air smelled of wet earth and burning peat. When they walked up to the bar, all the customers suddenly stopped talking, and a big man with black hair and a generous mustache waved them over to his table at the back.

Bud sized up the situation. There were only two tables in the back, and one was unoccupied. Standing with the big man were two shorter, rough-looking men, both red-haired. Bud studied them with growing unease, slipped his hand in his pocket, and fingered his revolver.

"You lookin' for me?" the big man asked.

Joe took a step toward him. "You Sean Garrity?"

"That I am. Are you General Joe Ring?"

"That would be me," Joe answered. "This is Captain Ryan."

Garrity gestured toward the other two men. "Standin' with me is Phineas Parker and George Dougherty, the Flying Column commanders for Galway."

Joe shook their hands, and Garrity gestured to the table. "Will you sit?"

Joe took the chair that put his back to the wall. Bud sat facing the entrance, so if there was trouble, he'd have Joe's back. A glass of beer appeared before him, and he took a sip.

Joe sent him a quick look, then focused on the big man across from him. "Garrity, I'd like to ask you a few questions."

Something warned Bud to watch the front door out of the corner of his eye. Joe took a sip of his beer and kept his hands on the table.

"So, General Ring, why are you here?" Garrity caught a quick glance from the other two men and leaned forward. "I have to tell you, General, that we are anti-treaty."

Slowly Bud eased his Bulldog out of his pocket.

"Actually," Joe said evenly, "that's not why I'm here. I'm investigating the murders of three former constables,

Patrick Cassidy, Tobias Gibbons, and John Gilmartin."

"Ah." Garrity released a breath, and all three men settled back in their chairs. "We thought you'd come here to enforce the treaty."

"No," Joe replied. Bud stuffed his revolver back in his pocket.

Joe took another sip of his beer. "Speakin' of the treaty," he said carefully, "how does Galway stand?"

After a slight hesitation Garrity cocked his head. "We're still sortin' out the details."

Joe nodded. "About these murders, Mr. Garrity. Who do you think is behind them?"

Garrity shrugged. "We have a pretty good idea, General, but we're not absolutely sure."

"Trucileers?"

An uncomfortable silence descended. "I understand that's the case in a lot of these killin's," Garrity said slowly, "but it's different here in Galway."

Joe gave him a long look. "How is it different?"

The big man rubbed his chin, then looked Joe straight in the eye. "We think the murders are the work of a pair of East Mayo IRA men."

Joe's mouth tightened. "Do you, now? I am commander of the East Mayo column. What are the names of these men?"

Garrity looked at his cohorts and leaned back in his chair. "Now why would I be givin' those names to you? These are loyal men, fightin' for Ireland. I say they acted in our best interests."

Joe stared straight at Garrity and tapped his fingers on the table. Garrity stared right back. Feeling the tension rise, Bud again fingered his Bulldog.

Garrity finally heaved a long sigh. "We know where these men are. We're bringin' them in. Is it all that necessary to know their names?"

"I can't be givin' the Brits reasons for comin' back," Joe explained. "Too many friends are dead. We have to end the violence."

It was Garrity's turn to stare at Joe while he considered his words.

Joe broke the silence. "What are you goin' to do with them, once you've brought 'em in?"

"Well," Garrity said slowly, "we'll ask them some questions. If they confess, they were the killers, we've already made arrangements." He leaned back and held Joe's gaze. "We'll be puttin' them on the first boat to America."

When Joe said nothing, Garrity sent him a questioning look. "Do you have a problem with that?"

Joe shifted in his chair and shot a glance at Bud, then returned his attention to Garrity and shrugged his shoulders. "As long as they're out of Ireland and no longer assassinating former constables, they're not my concern. But," he added, his voice hardening, "the killin' has to stop. Tell these men not to come back."

A grin broke across Garrity's pock-marked face. "Then we're on the same page, mate."

Joe smiled. "So we are."

"Now, about the treaty," Garrity continued. "We are not supportin' it."

"Earlier you sounded a bit unsure about that."

"Well we're not unsure," Garrity blustered. "Are we, mates?" he said over his shoulder. Both of his companions nodded.

Joe got to his feet, smiled again, and extended his hand. "Let me know what you find out about the murders and when you put these men on ships to America. If you need us, give me a call and we'll be back."

Garrity gripped his hand. "Said and done."

Relieved, Bud released his grip on the revolver and stood up as the men shook hands all around.

As they drove north out of Galway, Bud released a long breath. "I thought we were goin' to be in a shootout for sure," he said.

Joe grinned. "I didn't have that feelin', but Garrity was definitely on edge about the treaty. I thought for sure we'd have universal agreement now that the constables have been disbanded and the Tans are goin' back to England. What more could we ask?"

Bud shook his head and leaned back in his seat. "Yeah. What more could we ask?"

But when they reached Westport, they found a crowd of people milling about in front of the Mayo News office. Joe parked the car and he and Bud warily walked up to the fringes of the crowd.

"What's going on?" Bud asked an older man.

The man spun toward him. "Ye haven't heard then, have ye?"

"Heard what?"

"Jim Harris was shot last night. Killed right in his own home."

A cold hand gripped Bud's heart. "Jim Harris? *Constable* Jim Harris?"

"Aye, that's who. A bloody murder it was."

"Jesus," Joe breathed. "Oh, Jesus Christ."

Bud found he couldn't speak. *Not another one. Not Constable Harris. When is this going to end?*

Chapter Twenty-two

Counterattack

Joe groaned. "You and Harris were friends, weren't you?"

"Yeah," Bud said woodenly. "I was friendly with him, sure, but I wouldn't exactly say Constable Harris and I were friends. Still, I always thought he was a decent bloke."

Bud said nothing on the drive back to the Ring farm. When Joe parked the car, Rose flew out the front door, but she stopped short when she saw the look on Bud's face. "You've heard about Constable Harris, haven't you?"

He nodded. "Makes me sick, it does."

She stepped in close and hugged him. "Come inside, both of you. I'll make some tea."

Inside, they found an open newspaper spread out on the kitchen table. Bud clenched his fists when he read the headline. "IRA Sells Out."

"What's this?" Joe asked.

"It's a new newspaper," Walter said. "Called 'Western People.' It's decidedly anti-treaty."

"Is it, now?" Joe muttered.

Walter nodded. "It is. They're callin' the Mayo News a Bolshevik news organization."

"Bolshevik?"

Walter nodded, and Joe flipped to the editorial page, scanned it, and gritted his teeth. "Listen to this. 'To assert that any sensible Irishman went to London to get a Republic is mere hogwash. They might as well look for holy water in a Protestant church'."

"God and all the saints be helpin' us," Joe murmured. He looked up and took a deep breath. 'Tis plain they're after the Mayo News because it supports the treaty." He glanced at his brother. "Now we're name-calling, are we?"

Walter looked away, and Rose set out a ceramic teapot and five cups.

"Do you know who killed Constable Harris?" Bud asked.

Walter folded himself into a kitchen chair and stared at the newspaper on the table. "They're saying it was two Trucileers. Don't know their names."

Maggie joined him at the table. "We heard that attempted assassinations were carried out against former constables up in County Sligo, too."

Joe said nothing for a long minute while Rose poured out the tea. "Walter," he said suddenly. "We have to get the word out that this violence is unacceptable."

"And how do we do that, boyo?"

"We go over to Paddy Burke's and set up a meetin' with the Free State commanders."

"We're gettin' a lot of resistance recruitin' from anti-treaty men," Walter said. "They've taken to callin' themselves the 'New IRA'." Arrogant bunch they are. Last week Tom Ruane was recruitin' for your Free State army in Mayo and some anti-treaty rabble gave him some grief. Tom was shot. Only hit his hand, but it scared him."

Joe groaned. "We'll need to send the recruiters out in pairs."

"And make sure they're armed," Bud offered.

They sat drinking tea and not saying much until Jack Ring burst in. "Bad news," he panted. "Tom Ruane is dead. Willie Moran, he's the commander of the Bohola IRA ..." He took a quick breath. ". . . Well it seems Willie hunted Tom Ruane down and they argued about recruitment. Tom drew a revolver and shot him."

"Oh, Jesus," Joe muttered.

"There's more, I'm afraid," Jack said. "One of Moran's boys gunned Tom down in retaliation."

"Christ Jesus," Joe swore. "We've got a bloody war on our hands." He reached for a half-full bottle of whiskey, uncorked it, and splashed some into his tea. "We've got to get control of County Mayo. I need to drive the IRA Republicans out of the northern part of the county."

Bud held out his cup for some whiskey. "Who's in command of the anti-treaty Republicans up north?"

"Michael Kilroy."

"The same Michael Kilroy who led us at Kilmeena and Carrowkennedy?"

"The same."

A chill went up Bud's spine. He liked and respected Michael Kilroy. He was a brilliant tactician and would be a tough opponent. "I didn't know Kilroy was anti-treaty."

"Yeah, he is," Joe said. "His beliefs are uncompromised, and he's passionate about them."

Rose laid her hand on Bud's arm. "Bud, there's somethin' else you should know, and I don't know how to tell you."

"Tell me what?"

"When I went into Westport yesterday, I walked by Ryan Brothers tavern. It was all closed up."

Bud stared at her. "Closed? Did you find out why?"

"I asked around," she said, her voice quiet. "Your brothers have joined the new IRA."

Bud took a moment to let that sink in. "Actually, that doesn't surprise me."

Rose studied her teacup for a long moment, then looked up and met his eyes. "They joined Michael Kilroy's anti-treaty boys."

Bud felt like he'd been hit in the solar plexus with a cannonball.

"That does it!" Joe said suddenly. "Bud, let's meet day after tomorrow with all the Free State officers."

Bud said nothing.

"Bud?" Joe slid the whiskey bottle toward him. "Did you hear me?"

"Yeah, Joe, sure. Another meetin'."

* * *

The meeting was held around a scratched conference table in the Imperial Hotel ballroom in Westport. When the Ring brothers and Bud arrived, Castlebar's Sean McEion and his lieutenants rose from their chairs. Joe walked to the head of the table and looked down at a hand-drawn map of northern County Mayo someone had spread out on the table. Then he looked up and surveyed the other men.

"Where's Paddy Burke and his people?"

At that moment tall, round-shouldered Burke and two others strolled in. "Sorry we're late," Paddy murmured.

Joe didn't reply. Instead, he called the meeting to order. "First, I have to tell you that Eamon de Valera has stepped down as President of the Dail. He's now on the other side, servin' as the political head of the anti-treaty Sinn Fein group."

This announcement was met by audible groans. Joe didn't even look up. "Also steppin' down are Cathal Brugha and Austin Stack. Arthur Griffith replaces de Valera as President of the Dail."

A buzz went around the room. Joe waited for the chatter to die down and then made a second announcement. "I'm also sorry to report ..." He stopped and swallowed hard. "... report that yesterday Michael Collins, my friend and Chairman of the Provisional Government, was assassinated by IRA Republicans in Dublin."

The collective gasp stopped Bud's breath. "Michael Collins is dead?" someone called out.

Joe nodded and swallowed again. "Now to our own problem. We're up against Michael Kilroy and about seven hundred of his followers."

"What do you think they're about, mate?" someone called.

"They're expectin' to fight us the way we fought the English, with ambushes, skirmishes, blowin' up railway lines and bridges. We need to flush them out of their different barracks."

"What's your plan, Joe?" Sean McEion shouted.

"First I think we should issue a public condemnation of the assassinations of the constables. I've prepared a draft statement. Take a look at it, and if you agree, I'll have my brother Jack take it down to the Mayo Times." He pushed a piece of paper toward Sean for his review. "I also have an idea about cleanin' the new IRA Republicans out of County Mayo."

He pointed at the map spread across the table. "They're expectin' us to attack out of Westport. I propose that we surprise them." He pointed down at a spot, and the assembled men gathered around the map. "I propose we surprise them with a military-style attack from the rear. Start clearin' out their strongholds from a direction opposite to what they're expectin'."

He pointed again. "The Republicans have detained about ninety of our men in the Coast Guard station at Rosmoney. We'll use boats. I will land here ..." He stabbed his forefinger at a spot on the map, "on the beach north of the Quay, and attack. At the same time, Bud Ryan will land his men at the Quay and work his way inland to coordinate with my attack. Then we'll both link up with Sean McEion's forces coming west from Castlebar with cars, trucks, and other vehicles, includin' the armored car. Finally, we work our way back to Westport, drivin' the Republicans ahead of us and into the Ox Mountains."

"When will we do this?" Bud asked.

"In three days."

The meeting went on for another hour as the men discussed details, alternatives, and contingencies. Afterwards, Joe sent his brother Jack to get a copy of the Mayo Times before they headed back to the farm.

When they arrived, Bud and the Ring brothers trooped inside, and Jack opened the newspaper. "Oh, God almighty. It says here Cathal Brugha was killed in Dublin by Free State Forces."

"Cathal Brugha, too?" Bud exclaimed.

Walter peered at the article. "How old was Brugha?"

"Only fifty-one," Jack said.

Suddenly Bud found Rose's hand in his. "Let's take a walk," he whispered. She nodded, and they found their way to their favorite tree. He leaned back against the trunk and settled Rose between his knees, and they sat in silence for a few moments. Then he bent forward and kissed the back of her neck.

"I can tell you're upset, Bud. What's wrong?"

"It gets to you after a while," he said slowly. "All the killin'. All the dyin'." He tightened his arms around her. "I thought once we had our Republic, you and I could settle down and get on with our lives."

Rose shook his arm. "Don't be getting' depressed on me, Bud Ryan. We have to make this work. We have too much at stake for you to be goin' all soft on me."

"I'm sorry. It's just that I'm off to fight another battle, and this time I'll be fightin' against my own brothers."

"I know," she said. "I've already lost everyone but Maggie, not to mention the farm we've had for generations. We have to make this treaty work or the damned Brits will be back. Then where will we be?"

They sat in silence, watching the sun sink in the west, painting the sky peach and then purple. Then Rose twisted in his arms and kissed him. "Let's not waste any more time," she murmured.

Chapter Twenty-three

Attack from the Sea

The boat rolled, and Bud's head hit the wooden railing. He peered over the water at the shadows of the Quay and a tiny light in the distance as another swell rocked the vessel and he once more bumped his head against the rail. He gave up and stood erect. *How close are we to the Quay?* he wondered.

Stepping over and around the men, he made his way aft and stretched up to the pilot house. "How much longer?" he whispered.

"See that little light over there?"

"I see it."

"We should be there in about twenty minutes."

Bud made his way back to the bow and got ready to lead the men off the boat and down the concrete pier. He could hear the other boat but couldn't see its shadow, so as they approached, he ordered all lights extinguished, and to avoid a collision he kept the second boat 50 yards astern.

The tiny light grew larger, and the details of the Quay became more clearly defined. He looked toward the Coast Guard station, where everything was dark. *I hope Joe's boat is landing on the beach about now.*

They bumped up against the pier, and Bud jumped over the rail, tied off the boat, and led his men 30 yards down the pier. Then he held up his hand, and they stood in silence, waiting. The other boat reached the dock, and the men debarked. He led them all off the Quay and onto the dirt road leading north from the marina. Within a quarter mile he found the road leading through the woods to the Coast Guard station.

The station was dark, and the area around it was quiet. Bud divided his 60 men into squads and positioned them to cut off any escape when Joe Ring's men attacked.

Suddenly gunfire erupted from the far side of the station, and lights blazed on. Bud trained his eyes on the main entrance, but the double doors remained closed. Then the side doors burst open, and IRA gunmen stumbled outside.

Bud leaped to his feet. "Drop your guns," he yelled. "Drop your weapons! Now!"

Two men spun and leveled their rifles. Gunfire erupted to Bud's right, and both men crumpled to the ground. His men then advanced as voices from behind the station yelled for surrender.

After a long, tense silence, a while flag appeared out the side door, followed by a group of men with their hands raised over their heads. Bud walked past them and found Joe Ring.

"Nicely done," Joe said. "Any of your men hurt?"

"No. All fine."

Bud peered into the gloom as one of his men approached the front door. Something didn't feel right. Then all at once he understood. "Stop!" he screamed.

The man froze.

"Don't touch the door!"

Joe frowned. "What's wrong?"

"When you attacked from the other side, nobody came out the main entrance," Bud explained. "Instead, they all came out the side doors. And now I think I know why."

Joe stopped dead. "Yeah? Let's have a look."

Together with six men, they entered the station through a side door and worked their way to the front entrance. "Hold up!" Bud shouted. Cautiously he inched forward.

There in the middle of the floor, five feet back from the double front doors, lay three sticks of dynamite wired to a battery and a detonator. A pair of wires led from the detonator to the front doors.

"Why is the bomb so far away from the doors?" Joe wondered aloud.

"That's so when the doors open, the men comin' in get the full blast. Nasty bit of business," Bud muttered. "Joe, post guards on the other side of these doors and keep the men twenty feet away."

"Why?"

"In case I make a mistake," Bud said quietly.

"Jesus Chr—" Joe shouted to the men crowding behind him, "Get everyone out of here! We've a bomb that needs defusin'." He and the men trooped out, leaving Bud alone with the bomb.

He took a deep breath, knelt down, and rubbed his hands together. *Take your time. Take it slow and everything will be fine.* He inspected the wiring and the battery, then the detonator. To his relief, the apparatus was fairly crude and would be easy to defuse. The wires were connected to two pieces of copper foil placed close to each other, and these were attached to the doors so when they opened, the copper pieces would touch and activate the detonator. Gently he bent back the copper foil, then pulled a folding Army knife with a pair of clippers from his pocket and cut the wires.

Once he'd carefully removed the wires from the detonator, he began to breathe easier. He picked up the dynamite, battery, and detonator and shouldered open the double doors. The guards outside jumped.

"Clear the way to the beach for me," he said.

When the guards hesitated, he tipped his head toward the dynamite in his hand. Instantly they bolted ahead of him, shouting, "Clear a path! We have a bomb here."

The men parted like magic. When he reached the water's edge, he waded out thigh-deep and carefully submerged the bomb assembly. When he waded back out, Joe met him at the water's edge. "My God," he breathed. "Nice work."

Bud showed him the dripping package. "Someone should take this apart and dry out the dynamite."

"Right." Joe swallowed. "We found about ninety Free State prisoners back there."

Bud just looked at him. "What are you going to do with the Republicans?"

A smile broke across his face. "I thought a little poetic justice might be in order."

"How do you mean?"

"I asked the fifteen Free Staters who've been here the longest to stay and guard the Republicans. If they abused any of our men ..." Joe's voice trailed off, and Bud nodded. "Sends a message to any other Republicans who are holdin' our men as prisoners."

Joe grinned. "When we get back to Westport, I'll have the Mayo News publish a bloomin' fancy article about what you did."

Bud chuckled. "Very poetic, Joe."

"Get your men together," Joe said. "We have to march east to meet Sean McEion and his boys."

The sun was just coming up when their combined forces marched toward Castlebar. Near the town of Tawnyman, Bud heard motor vehicles coming from the opposite direction. From the crest of a hill, they watched a Ford automobile, followed by a Chesley troop carrier and the armored car, grind toward the town with 15 or so cars and trucks lined up behind it.

Joe waved the convoy to a stop, and Sean McEion jumped out of the Ford and walked straight up to him. "We formed up north of Castlebar," he reported. "As we approached the town, the Republicans panicked, burned their barracks, and fled. I left some of my men to garrison the town."

Joe studied the armored car. "What do you call that beast?"

"We call it 'The Big Fella'."

"Would you have room for our troops in your convoy?"

Sean hid a smile. "There's room for everyone."

"Bud," Joe said suddenly. "Get your troops into one group of vehicles and take the right flank guardin' our movement from the north. Sean, I want you to go south and stay on my left flank. Both of you stay close enough so that if you need support, I can send men. I'll lead the main troops in the middle, and we'll press on into Westport."

It took 15 minutes to get organized, during which Joe spread out a map on the hood of the Ford. "Bud, see this road parallel to the Castlebar to Westport road? I want you to stay on it. Sean, your route is a little trickier. You'll be out in those fields, so try to keep up."

Both men nodded, and Joe continued. "As we go west, we'll run into clumps of Republicans. Most will flee, and if they do, let them go. But if they shoot at you, attack them. I want to be in Westport by this evening. Any questions?"

Sean and Bud glanced at each other and shook their heads.

Bud found his command car, and he and his lieutenants led their caravan north, then turned toward Westport. The road went through the middle of an area just outside Westport called Carrowtootagh. The main street of the town was only a block and a half long, its primary features a wooden church with a single bell tower topped by a cross, a small general store, and a post office.

As they got closer, they encountered some gunfire. Bud sent Mike Kelly and his boys on a swing around to the other end of the main street, kept Dick Byrne's men in place, and took the bulk of his own unit and the Chesley troop carrier with the Jennings machine gun to the south side.

The best advantage the town defenders would have was from the church tower. When they reached the church, Bud stood up. "Come out and show yourselves," he shouted.

His demand was met with gunfire. He circled behind the Chesley and spread the men behind the other vehicles. Dick Byrne led his troops into the western end of the town, while Kelly's men fought a gun battle from the east side against the defenders in the bell tower.

Bud told the Jennings crew to assemble the gun and point it at the tower. They raked it with machine gun fire until the return fire ceased; then Mike Kelly stood up, waved, and entered the town.

When another gun fight erupted, Bud pulled out his Bulldog and ordered the men forward. Everyone, including the machine gun crew, funneled in between the post office and the general store. Bud halted their attack at that point and directed the Jennings crew to get ready. The firing came from the direction of Dick Byrne's troops, and Bud saw that some Republicans were shooting from a horse stable.

When the machine gun was in position, he stood up. "We've got you surrounded," he shouted. "Come on out."

Instead, they opened fire. Bud dropped to the ground, and then the Jennings erupted. Suddenly all the shooting stopped, and Carrowtootagh fell silent. He led four men across the street into the barn, where he found six dead bodies. He recognized the Porter brothers and their cousin, Peter Flood, and his heart sank. They'd been regulars at Ryan Brothers tavern.

This is tragic. There was no need to die over this treaty.

Mike Kelly reported that the four men in the church tower were all dead. "One was Joe Walsh. I didn't know the others."

Bud said nothing for a full minute. Then he issued his orders. "Leave six men and one of the cars. Take the bodies to the church and find the priest, then get in the car and catch up with us."

In the next hour, he met Joe and Sean just east of Westport and told them about Joe Walsh and the others. Joe Ring looked off to one side and swore. Then he straightened and looked straight at Bud. "It's too late to launch an attack on Westport. Besides, I want to give them a chance to surrender. We'll move in tomorrow morning."

"What about our families?" Sean asked.

"I want no one alone in the town until we clear

Westport. If anyone wants to spend some time in their homes, go in groups."

Then Joe touched Bud's arm. "Why don't you come back to our farm? We need to do some plannin', and maybe Rose and Maggie can tell us what's been goin' on in town."

Bud nodded, then found himself wondering about his brothers, Mike and Kevin. Maybe Maggie or Rose would know something about them.

Chapter Twenty-four

Preparing for Ballina

All the way back to Joe Ring's farmhouse, Bud thought about what had happened that day and worried about what would happen tomorrow in Westport. He found himself assessing the toll the struggle for Irish independence was taking on those he cared the most about, his brothers Kevin and Mike, and on Rose. He didn't want to fight; he wanted to be with her. He wanted time to build a life with her. He felt her absence like a sharp rock in his gut.

When the car emptied, he strode into the Rings' farmhouse and found Rose in the kitchen, pulled her close, and held her. "God, I miss you," he breathed. "I want this to stop so we can be together."

She looked up at him with tears in her eyes, but she didn't speak. When Joe entered the house, he immediately walked over to her. "Rose, Westport seems quiet, but that might not mean anything. Do you have any sense of what's goin' on in town?"

"I do, actually."

Maggie turned from the kitchen stove where she'd been scrambling some eggs. "There are some anxious people in Westport."

"Anxious, how?" Joe asked.

"Well, the loudest anti-treaty Republicans have left town." Rose took the spatula from her sister so she could hug Walter.

"Some went into hiding," Rose added.

"And some," Maggie continued, her voice hardening, "have decided to take a ship for America. But most of them have left town to join Michael Kilroy and his IRA men."

Joe settled into one of the chairs around the kitchen table. "Any idea where Kilroy is gathering his troops?"

Maggie nodded and turned back to the stove. "We heard lots of different things in town. One name that kept comin' up was Ballina."

"Ballina!" Walter shot. "Ballina's almost up in County Sligo."

"Do you know how many men have gone to Ballina?" Joe

pursued.

Maggie shook her head.

Joe thought for a moment, then turned to his brother, Jack. "Take the Ford into town," he said shortly. "See what you can learn."

Before Jack reached the door, Joe stopped him. "If you find out that the Republicans have all left town, and you think it's safe, send all the men we left in Westport home. Tell them we'll be marchin' on Ballina in three days."

Jack touched the visor of his hat. "I'll tell them."

"Ballina," Joe muttered. "It makes sense to have everyone gather in north County Mayo. This is typical Kilroy—disperse, then reassemble."

"Do you think the Republicans attacked any of the troops we left in Castlebar?" Bud asked.

Joe stared off into space before answering. Finally, he shook his head. "Kilroy is smarter than that. He knows I'll come after him, so it would make more sense to gather his men and make a defensive stand. They can defend Ballina in front of the town, and if things go badly, they can fall back into the town."

"And," Bud added, "if necessary, they can escape into the Ox Mountains."

"Not a lot different from Kilmeena," Walter observed. "Same tactics."

Joe looked up at the ceiling and tented his fingers. "Kilroy will stay with what works. If Jack confirms that all the Republicans have left Westport, then we should expect an ambush on the road to Ballina. Maybe find some obstacles in our way to slow us down."

Maggie began laying out plates and silverware. "Somethin' else you should know is that one of the women in town was braggin' that the Republicans now have an armored car. They captured it from somewhere."

"It used to be called Ballinalee," Rose added. "They renamed it The Rose of Lough Gill."

"They named it after a lake?" Walter asked, his tone incredulous.

Rose nodded. "That's what we heard."

"We have an armored car, too," Joe said thoughtfully. "Let's see what else Jack finds out in town."

Before the brothers sat down to supper, Bud and Rose slipped outside. Bud could smell rain in the air, so they went into the barn, where they climbed up to the loft and nestled in the straw. Rose settled into his arms and looked up at him. "How much longer is this fightin' going to go on, Bud?"

He sighed. "I wish I knew. Our Free Army is doin' pretty well here in County Mayo, but it looks like we're goin' to fight Michael Kilroy up in Ballina."

"I want this to end, Bud. I want us to start makin' some

plans."

"Rose, you know I feel the same."

"Maggie's goin' daft worryin' about Walter. I keep tellin' myself you have military experience, that you know how to stay alive, but I can't help worryin' about you." She tipped her head up and kissed him.

"Try not to worry, Rose. It does no good. When I'm out with the troops I don't want to be thinkin' about you worryin' over me."

"All Maggie talks about is Walter, how much she wants the two of them to go to America and leave all this violence behind."

He tightened his arms around her. "Joe Ring knows what he's doin'. I don't always agree with him, but he gave orders not to engage the Republicans in Westport if they didn't stand and fight." He thought for a moment. "But," he said slowly, "if we don't fight them, this war could drag on forever."

"Oh, don't say that. Don't even think it."

"Joe usually makes good tactical decisions. The troops look up to him. They're calling' us 'Ring's Own'."

Thunder rumbled overhead, then the patter of raindrops on the barn roof increased to a downpour. In silence they clung to each other and listened to the storm until they heard a car pull into the yard. When Bud peeked out, he saw Jack Ring and an unfamiliar man disappear into the house.

"We've got to go in, Rose. Somethin's happening." They made a dash for the back door, and when they entered the house, they found the stranger shaking hands with Joe and Walter Ring. Rose brushed the rain off her clothes, and the stranger tipped his hat to her. Then he reached to shake Bud's hand.

"You must be Bud Ryan. Jack's told me a lot about you."

"Yeah? Who--?"

"I'm Bert Simmons. I command the Free State unit from Athlone. General Lawlor ordered us and the unit from Claremorris to join you for the assault on Ballina."

Bud shot a look at Jack. "So, the girls were right. Kilroy is gathering his men at Ballina?"

Jack nodded.

Joe buttonholed Simmons. "How many men does Kilroy have up there?"

"We think about a hundred and fifty, give or take maybe ten, and they're armed with rifles and a couple of machine guns. And," he added, "they have an armored car."

Joe frowned. "How reliable is your information?"

"We think it's pretty accurate," Simmons said, cocking his head.

"Maggie," Joe said, "could you serve up some supper for

us?"

"Sure," Maggie and Rose said together.

Bud took a seat at the table with the other four men, and over a platter of Maggie's scrambled eggs and a pot of tea they discussed how they could combine the three forces for an attack on Ballina. When Joe insisted on a three-day pause to rest his troops, Bud's heart jumped, and he sent Rose a significant look. *That could be just time enough.*

While the discussion went on and on, he watched Rose move about the kitchen, her red pigtails swinging while she worked, the way she led with her chin when she walked. When she bent near him, he could see the sprinkling of freckles across her nose. That dissolved the last bit of hesitation he felt.

"Joe, could I borrow the car?"

"Sure. Where would you be off to?"

He ignored the question and reached for Rose's hand. "Come with me. Walter, Maggie, I want you to come with us."

Walter and Maggie stared at each other. Rose lifted her chin. "Where are we going?"

Bud said nothing until he'd bundled them all into the car and drove out of the farmyard and Rose again asked, "Where are we going?"

"We're going to see Father Blaney."

Her eyes widened. "What? Why?"

"We're goin' to get married." He caught Walter's eyes in the rearview mirror. "And you and Maggie are our witnesses."

"Really?" Rose said breathlessly. "You mean *now*?" She slid closer to him. "Aren't you even goin' to ask me if I'll marry you?" she said with laughter in her voice.

"I already asked you, months ago, and you said yes. So, we're not goin' to wait any longer."

"Bud, stop! We need to go back to the farm so I can put on a nicer dress. I can't get married in this, it's too plain."

Bud parked in front of the rectory and looked over at her. "There is no way you could look any better to me. Let's do this here and now. I won't wait any longer."

A pink flush suffused Rose's face, and he tried not to smile. *That's the first time I've ever seen my darling Rose blush.*

The housekeeper answered the rectory door and invited them into the waiting room. Then Father Blaney appeared in his black cassock and collar. "Ah, 'tis Rose Ludden and her young man, Bud Ryan. What can I do for you?"

"Rose and I want to get married," Bud blurted. "You published the banns months ago, and now we want you to conduct the ceremony."

"Now? Tonight?"

"Now," Bud answered decisively. "Tonight."

The priest nodded, disappeared into the rectory, and emerged with a missal. He opened it, then began to read the words of the ceremony.

In the middle of making their vows, Bud got the shakes. It was one thing to get married on a clear summer's day in a peaceful town with a congregation of invited friends watching. It was another to do it in the middle of a war he hadn't asked for and didn't want. *Jesus, in three days, Rose could be a widow.*

He shook off the thought, and at the conclusion of the ceremony he bent to kiss Rose and hugged Maggie. Walter pumped his hand. They signed the registry, thanked Father Blaney, and climbed back into the Ford. Bud then headed straight back to the Ring farm.

"What are you two newlyweds going to do now?" Walter ventured.

Bud kept his eyes on the road. "I'm takin' you and Maggie back to the farm. Then Rose and I are goin' to Galway and rent a cottage on the beach. I'll be back in Westport in time to leave for Ballina with the rest of the convoy."

Rose snuggled her head onto his shoulder and said nothing.

Back at the house, Maggie helped Rose pack a small

suitcase while Bud found Joe and explained. "It's about time," Joe said warmly. "Congratulations. Ye'll want the Ford, so take it."

Jack slapped him hard on the back. "Congratulations, mate. When this fightin's over, we'll have a proper celebration."

Maggie stretched up to kiss his cheek, then folded Rose into an embrace. "Wish us luck," Rose whispered.

"You know I do," Maggie murmured. "Always."

With a final wave goodbye, Bud put Rose in the car, climbed into the driver's seat, and pointed it south.

Chapter Twenty-five

Storming Ballina

The morning Bud and Rose returned from Galway, they drove into a frenzy of military activity around Joe Ring's headquarters at the Imperial Hotel in Westport. When Bud stepped out of the car, Jack Ring raced up, out of breath. "Bud, where have you been?" He didn't wait for an answer. "Never mind. Drive on over to headquarters, find Mike Kelly, and take command of your men."

Bud stared at him. "Now? I'm just back from my honeymoon, Jack. Rose hasn't even had time to unpack."

"Oh, well sure, I understand," Jack acknowledged. "But this is important, so maybe Rose could catch a ride out to the farm with someone else."

While Bud was parking the car, his lieutenants, Mike Kelly and Dick Byrne, found him. "Have you got your uniform with you?" Mike asked.

Bud jerked his thumb over his shoulder. "It's in the car."

"Well, get it and put it on. We're about to leave for Ballina."

"Ballina? Now?"

"Yes, now," Mike said. "Come on."

Bud grabbed their luggage and started for the hotel. "What's goin' on?" Rose asked in alarm.

"I have to go, Rose. We're makin' our attack on Ballina. Could you find a ride back to the farm?"

"Sure." She kissed him, and he bolted into the men's room to don his uniform. When he emerged, he found Mike again.

"Did you get our orders at the planning meetin' this morning?" he asked.

"Be sure that I did."

"And?" Bud waited impatiently.

"A Jennings machine gun crew was assigned to us. There's one machine gun crew assigned to each of our five units."

"Where did we get all this firepower?"

"Dublin's been gettin' money from America, donations from the Irish who have emigrated. The Dublin folks were able to buy new arms, and they sent us a huge shipment."

Bud nodded.

"When we move out," Mike continued, "we'll be second in line, just behind Joe Ring's unit."

"Right." He caught sight of Rose, standing with Maggie as Father Blaney blessed the men. He caught her eye and waved. *This is surely one hell of a way to start a marriage.*

Dick Byrne now sat behind the automobile's steering wheel, so Bud climbed in the back with Mike Kelly, and the car moved forward to join the line of vehicles.

"Joe Ring's unit with the armored car is ahead of us," Dick explained. "We're next in line. Sean McEion's boys from Castlebar are behind us, along with Bert Simmons and his men from Athlone. The Claremorris lads, that's Tom Slatterly's unit, are guardin' our rear."

"How will we be deployed when we get to Ballina?"

Dick caught his eye in the rearview mirror. "Joe's unit will take the middle. We're to swing wide left to block any escape from town on the western flank, and Sean McEion's men will secure the eastern flank."

Bud nodded for him to go on.

"Our last two units will join Joe Ring in the center and fight with him on the direct assault into Ballina from the south."

Just then the car rolled past the shuttered Ryan

Brothers tavern, and Bud caught his breath. It took a moment for him to refocus on the job at hand. "Mike, do we know what we're facing?"

"We think Michael Kilroy has about a hundred and fifty men in Ballina. We have over two hundred, so we outnumber them."

Bud pressed his lips together. *Being outnumbered means nothing, but Joe must know that.*

They rolled out of Westport at a brisk 40 miles per hour, and Mike continued his explanation. "If Kilroy abandons Ballina, he'll be blocked by our flanking units. His only choice will be to retreat into the Ox Mountains near the Lough Talt lake. If the battle moves into the mountains, we should be ready to join the main assault."

The weather looked threatening as the convoy motored on out of the grass-covered coastal mountains that surrounded Westport and descended onto the rocky Irish central plains. Small stone farmhouses with thatched roofs dotted the countryside; modern, wood-framed farmhouses stood on the more successful farms. Bud suddenly remembered Cromwell's general, Edmund Ludlow, who in 1651 had said, "Ireland is a country where there is not water enough to drown a man, wood enough to hang one, nor earth enough to bury him."

Today Bud didn't feel much like laughing.

The landscape was much the same through Islandeady, Castlebar, Strade, and Foxford. In the countryside, cattle picked their way around rocky outcroppings to find grass. Small villages dotted the roads where curious residents lined the streets to watch the military convoy roll past. As they drove by, some of the children lining the town streets waved green, white, and orange Free State flags. Their parents stood by, curious but silent.

After Attymass, the road was clear and the weathered, rounded foothills of the Ox Mountain range were visible. Here the line of military vehicles slowed to a stop.

Bud peered out his window. "Dick, find out what's holdin' us up."

Byrne slid his long legs out of the Ford and craned his neck. "Looks like we're here," he said when he climbed back behind the wheel. "I can see the town. The Ring brothers are directin' traffic off the road."

The column inched forward until Joe Ring appeared at the car window. "Bud, head across this field and cut the Ballina to Crossmolia road, then set your command post on the hill and connect with Tom Slatterly's boys from Claremorris. I'll be attackin' from the center. As the situation allows, advance your men forward into Ballina and kill or capture as many Republicans as you can. We have to take control of these rebel strongholds."

They left the road and bumped over a pasture until Bud spied the low hill overlooking the town. Dick parked the car, and Bud formed his men into an arc looking down on what would be the battlefield. He positioned the machine gun in the center and interspersed men carrying grenades throughout, then watched the rest of the convoy find their places on both sides of the armored car.

A sudden sense of dread swept over him. *Are my brothers down there? For certain I never thought I'd be facing them on opposite sides of a battlefield.*

He could see Michael Kilroy's armored car facing south, poised to take on Joe Ring's Free State army, and he clenched his fists. He desperately wished Kevin and Mike were back at the tavern, lugging cartons of whiskey up from the basement or swiping a cloth along the mahogany countertop. A chill swept over him.

Suddenly he heard Joe Ring's voice. "Fire!"

The center of the line opened up with a single volley, accompanied by the rat-tat-tat of a machine gun. Bud turned to his men. "Fire!"

The other three units also fired a single volley into the town, accompanied by short bursts from the machine guns. A stream of vehicles and men escaped out of the unthreatened northern end of Ballina, moving northeast toward Carrowmore into the foothills of the Ox Mountains.

Bud caught sight of sunlight glinting off a device carried by three men in the town below. "Look at that," he called. "That's a machine gun. I can't tell if it's a Jennings or a Vickers."

"What does it matter?" someone shouted.

"A Vickers takes longer to set up, so we might be able to catch up with them before they can get it ready." Below him he watched Joe and Jack Ring enter the town on foot, using the armored car for cover. Walter Ring advanced with Tom Slatterly's men, and Bud ordered his men forward toward Ballina. But instead of going into the now-deserted town, he directed them to the north side of the village. Just as they reached the village limits, he saw Kilroy's armored vehicle roll backwards out of the town.

Joe Ring's Nationalist troops answered the gunfire from Kilroy's retreating Republicans with short bursts of rifle and machine gun fire. Suddenly Kilroy's armored car began firing its turret machine gun at them, and immediately the Free State's advancing armored vehicle rotated its own turret and began firing its machine gun back at Kilroy's car.

Good Holy God, it's turning into a battle between the armored cars.

Bud watched the two armored cars blast away at each other. Bullets bounced off both vehicles until Kilroy's gun unexpectedly stopped firing and the car veered off to the right.

"Face left!" Bud shouted to his men. "Stop those lads runnin' into the hills." In the ensuing gun battle he watched some of his own men go down.

The battle between the two armored cars raged until Joe Ring's vehicle sped up and fired its machine gun into the back of Kilroy's armored car. Kilroy's vehicle reacted by backing up and ramming Joe's armored car, firing its machine gun at point blank range. Joe's gun went silent.

Oh, Christ. We needed that gun.

As he watched, one of Joe's men ran forward and rolled a grenade under Kilroy's armored car. The resulting blast ended its role in the battle.

Bud ordered his machine gun crew to fire into the fleeing horde of Kilroy's IRA men. Some zig-zagged to avoid bullets; others fell. But when his own troops moved northeast toward Carrowmore, they discovered that Kilroy had dug trenches and planted landmines to slow their advance. Small parties of snipers fired at them.

Bodies littered the fields behind Ballina, in front of Carrowmore, and well up into the mountain passes. Machine gun fire pinned Bud's troops down, and while Joe Ring's men were funneling into the first pass, Bud heard someone shout his name. He turned to see Dick Kelly motioning to him.

"Come with me," Dick shouted.

"But we have an attack goin' on!"

"Just come!" Kelly yelled. He led Bud about 50 yards away from the battle and pointed down at a body. "One of my men said this was your brother."

Bud's entire body went cold. He knelt beside the still form on the ground and leaned in close. *Oh, my God, it's Kevin.* His face was grey, and blood seeped from a hole in his chest.

He felt sick. *I hate this war.*

Very slowly he got to his feet and moved toward the sound of gunfire. Part of him didn't care if he got killed. All at once something that felt like a fist smacked him in the shoulder, and he fell to his knees. When he checked his upper body, he found a small hole in the shoulder of his uniform, and blood was oozing from the wound. He got to his feet and scanned the battlefield.

When he could focus on his surroundings, he saw that Joe Ring's Free State Army was pushing Kilroy's men deeper into the mountains. Machine guns and rifles continued to fire, but gradually the shooting slowed and then stopped. A surreal quiet descended.

He found Mike Kelly. "Report?" he asked, his voice flat.

Kelly glanced up. "Captain, you've been hit!"

He glanced down at his bloody sleeve and nodded. "It's

not bad. I need your report."

Kelly looked at him oddly. "Sean McEion's boys attacked the command center. Michael Kilroy is dead. His body is over there." He gestured behind him.

For a moment the words made no sense. Then he jerked to attention.

"And?"

"There's more news, Bud. Don't know how to say this, but ... a little while ago Joe and Jack Ring walked into an ambush. They were movin' forward, callin' for surrender, when a machine gun opened up on them. Joe Ring is dead."

Bud's senses began to swim and his vision dimmed. *Pull yourself together. Concentrate.* "What about Jack Ring?" he managed.

"Jack wasn't hurt."

Bud nodded.

"What are your orders, Captain Ryan?"

"I'm going to find out who's in charge now and what we plan to do next. Take command until I return."

He picked his way to the center of the formation and stopped one of the men. "Who's in charge?" he asked.

The man pointed to a knot of men on his left. Bud walked over to find Jack Ring leading a discussion of some kind. The front of his uniform was spattered with blood.

Jack turned toward him. "Bud, thank God you're here!

The Republicans have posted snipers along the mountain passes to cover their retreat, like we did at Kilmeena. We're going to fall back and dig in. Get your men off the battlefield and back to safety. And get your shoulder looked at!"

Bud nodded and turned away. When he returned to his men, he ordered a retreat, then tramped back to where Kevin lay. He ordered two of his men to carry his brother's body to the Chesley troop carrier and lay him in the back. Then he stripped off his tunic and got one of the men to bandage his bloody shoulder. He didn't think his wound was serious until he found he could no longer use his left arm.

As he rebuttoned his shirt he looked up to see a group of men carrying Joe Ring's body. They laid Joe in the Chesley next to Kevin.

He felt cold and dead inside, all the fight drained out of him. Dazed, he stared at the mountains in the distance. *Where is my brother Mike? Is he hurt? Is he on the run?*

Does he know about Kevin?

Walter and Margaret "Maggie" Ludden Ring

Chapter Twenty-six

Hard Decisions

The Chesley arrived in Westport with the bodies of his brother, Kevin, and Joe Ring. Bud, who had ridden with the driver, swung down and watched a crowd gather in front of the Imperial Hotel. Dick Byrne emerged from the convoy following the Chesley and walked up to him.

"I heard you got shot, Captain. How are you doing?"

"Me, I'm fine," Bud said shortly. "Could you make sure my brother's body gets to the morgue?"

"Of course. I'm right sorry about Kevin, Bud."

Then a familiar figure stepped out of the crowd. "Bud!" Rose stiffened at the sight of his blood-stained tunic. "Oh, Bud, you're wounded!" She stood on tiptoe and kissed him, then put her arms around him, careful not to jostle his arm. "What happened to you?"

He side-stepped the question. "'Tis not all bad, Rose. My arm's not workin' like it should, so I'm thinkin' I'm partially paralyzed. If so, what with my bad hip and all, I'll probably be discharged."

He took a deep breath and tipped his chin toward the Chesley. "My brother Kevin's body is in the back of that truck."

Her face went ashen. "Kevin? Oh, my God, Bud, not Kevin!" she sobbed. "My heart's breakin'."

"Joe Ring's body is in there, too."

Her hand covered her mouth. "Oh, no." She laid her head on his chest. "Was your brother Mike with Kevin when ..."

Bud looked out across the crowd. "I don't know," he said, his voice quiet. "I never saw Mike. Can't stop thinkin' about him, though."

Rose took his good arm. "Come with me. You should see Dr. Reilly about your wound."

On the way to the doctor they passed Ryan Brothers tavern, and Bud hesitated. "I thought about reopening this place," he said slowly. "Maybe when Mike shows up, we could run it together."

Rose said nothing, just squeezed his hand.

Dr. Reilly cleaned his wound and put in some stitches. "You can't move your arm, I gather," he said. "Not surprising, considering where that bullet tore into your shoulder."

Bud said nothing. When they left Dr. Reilly's office, Rose spotted Maggie. Her sister was crying. Walter draped his arm around Bud's good shoulder. "Come to the house tonight, Bud. We'll be havin' a wake for Kevin."

"We'll be there."

They walked on to St. Mary's rectory and made arrangements for Kevin's funeral. There was still no sign of Mike, so Bud asked Rose to find Jack Ring and collect Walter and Maggie for the drive out to the Ring farm.

While Maggie and Rose fixed something for supper, Bud lay on the couch, wondering about Mike, then he tried to stop thinking and drifted off. He woke up just as the first mourners knocked on the door and left a bouquet of roses for the family.

* * *

Joe Ring's funeral was the biggest event ever held in Westport. The funeral for Kevin a day later was small and private, just Rose, Maggie, and Walter and Jack Ring.

Bud still had heard no word from Mike, and he couldn't help but wonder if his brother was still alive. If he was, why didn't he come home to Westport?

In the middle of Kevin's funeral service, he had a sudden thought. *Maybe Mike was sick to death of this civil war, fighting against each other and killing our own countrymen. Maybe he's fled to America. But would his brother do a daft thing like that without even saying goodbye?*

Kevin Ryan and Joe Ring were buried at Aughaval Cemetery. The day after the services, Bud and Rose reopened Ryan Brothers tavern and moved in upstairs.

A week later, what was left of the Ring and the Ryan families gathered around a table in the tavern. Walter cleared his throat and took Maggie's hand. "We've lost almost everything," he said quietly. "The Ludden family, Kevin Ryan, and my brother Joe. We've lost everything except for ourselves."

"The Hawking Land Trust made sure we lost our land, too," Bud added. "Most of us Catholic families work the land, but those damn penal laws are wipin' them out. If the land is divided among all the children when their father dies, 'tis guaranteed after a few generations Catholic lands will be watered down to just small subsistence farms, like the Mills farm."

"The penal laws didn't apply to English Protestants," Rose said quietly. "The Land Trust farms compete with our Catholic farms for beef and wool, so it's to their advantage to lower their prices and force us out of business."

Bud retrieved a bottle of whiskey and opened it. "When I got back from the war, I went to the Land Trust office in Westport, lookin' for work so Rose and I could get married. They turned me down flat, and I know t'was because I'm Catholic."

Walter shook his head. "And s'posin' you and Rose have children. The Land Trust funds all the private Protestant schools, but Catholics like us are left with only the public schools."

"And the public schools are gettin' to be truly shabby," Maggie said, pressing her lips together. "T'will only get worse. Our schools will be no competition for the private schools."

"Eamon de Valera is leadin' the opposition to the Free State," Jack Ring offered. "Both Arthur Griffith and Michael Collins, the men who signed the treaty that established our Republic, are dead. Michael Kilroy is dead. And I'm thinkin' this civil war is far from over."

"Maggie and I are both sick of it," Walter added. He stopped talking long enough to sip some of the whiskey Bud had poured. Then he leaned forward and again took Maggie's hand. "I've got two steerage passages to the United States. We want to go to America before they pass any laws keepin' the Irish out. Father Blaney is marryin' us next

Tuesday, and then we're goin' to take a ship away from here and start a new life."

Maggie laid her hand on Rose's arm. "We want you and Bud to come with us."

A long silence fell. Finally, Rose exchanged a long glance with Bud and turned to Walter and her sister. "Bud and I will be stayin' here in Ireland and runnin' Ryan Brothers tavern. If Bud's brother Mike turns up, maybe we'll reconsider goin' to America."

"Walter," Bud asked, "what are you goin' to do in America?"

"Only three kinds of jobs are open to the Irish in America--law enforcement, bein' a fireman, or workin' for the railroad. We're headin' to a place in Indiana called Hammond. 'Tis an Irish community, and it's got one of the biggest railroad switchin' yards in the country. I'm goin' to get me a job on one of the railroads."

Rose turned to look at Maggie. "This means you'll be leavin' me," she said tearfully. "And you're my only sister."

"I'll write you every week," Maggie promised. "We sail next Wednesday after the weddin'. Jack has decided to come, too," she added. "He keeps talkin' about goin' to California."

They sat without speaking for a long minute, then lifted their glasses and, with tears in their eyes, they silently toasted each other.

THE END

Epilogue

Bud kept Mike Ryan's room at the tavern ready for him, but his brother never returned to Westport.

General Anthony Lawlor took over the Free State forces for Joe Ring, added another unit to that army, and increased recruitment. Stories of atrocities committed by the new IRA emerged from the various detention barracks across all 26 counties of the Free State. Republican ambushes were as common as the Free State firing squads organized by General Lawlor. The civil war may have claimed more Irish lives than the war for Irish independence.

A ceasefire was finally enacted on May 24, 1923, eight months after Joe Ring had been killed. Although both sides agreed to the ceasefire terms, random acts of violence continued for years.

Bud and Rose Ryan operated Ryan Brothers tavern under the same name. However, eventually the scars of the Civil War dictated that another tavern open on the other side of Westport's business district. Ryan Brothers tavern came to be known as a Free State tavern; the Brass Rail catered to Republicans.

Walter Ring did find a job on the Nickel Plate Railroad in Hammond, Indiana, where he and Maggie settled and raised three children: Mary Patricia, Catherine Veronica, and Walter Bernard Ring. Walter Bernard Ring is the author's father.

Rose and Maggie never saw each other again, but they corresponded regularly for over 50 years.

And Jack Ring found his wife, Margaret, in Los Angeles, where he became a lineman for Southern California Edison and raised a family of two girls, Rachel and Fiona.

Also by the Author

Red Sky in the Morning